HE

THE SPUR LINE

Tom Rhodes only wanted to run the horse ranch he'd inherited. His years as a peace officer had given him more than his fill of trouble, but it seemed it just wouldn't go away. He found his land was coveted by the Sweetwater Cattle Combine. Worse still, their ramrod, Manolito, was willing to kill to get it. Rhodes couldn't understand why Manolito wanted it so badly and answers weren't forthcoming. That is, not until he strapped on his gun again and took on the Combine's posse of thugs.

MIKE STALL

THE SPUR LINE

Complete and Unabridged

LINFORD
Leicester

First published in Great Britain in 2004 by
Robert Hale Limited
London

First Linford Edition
published 2005
by arrangement with
Robert Hale Limited
London

British Library CIP Data

Stall, Mike
    The spur line.—Large print ed.—
Linford western library
1. Western stories
2. Large type books
I. Title
823.9′14 [F]

ISBN 1–84395–777–9

Published by
F. A. Thorpe (Publishing)
Anstey, Leicestershire

Set by Words & Graphics Ltd.
Anstey, Leicestershire
Printed and bound in Great Britain by
T. J. International Ltd., Padstow, Cornwall

This book is printed on acid-free paper

PROLOGUE

It sounded as if the battle of Antietam was being fought in the Golden Slipper saloon, Tom Rhodes thought — and corrected himself instantly. The sound was nothing like it; just the same there was fear in his belly, gripping like a vice. For all that he walked to the sound of the gunfire.

He paused by the swing-doors, his hand reaching instinctively for the Colt on his right hip, and then he stopped himself. It was just a drunk with a pair of six-guns and a bellyful of rotgut whiskey.

It had gone quiet but, peering round the door, Rhodes saw that the guns were still drawn and in the hands of Toby Freas, a farmer with a quarter section round Standing Trees way. No gunfighter at all, a plain sodbuster with a plain wife, who'd died in childbed last

1

month. And by all accounts the bank was about to foreclose on him this month. He had something to let rip for.

But a sodbuster's bullet can kill you just as dead as any hired gunman's. Maybe he ought to go back to the office for a shotgun? He could shoot him from the doorway then. He knew some lawmen wouldn't hesitate to do that. Drunk or sober, a man shooting up the place was a man safer dead. But Rhodes liked to sleep nights. He entered the saloon, his six-gun still in its holster.

Freas turned, guns still in his hands but aimed high. The whiskey hadn't relaxed him. His face was that of a man in hell, tears wet on his cheeks.

'Goddamn you!' he said.

'Easy, Toby,' Rhodes said, moving very slowly now. 'Take it easy. You haven't killed anybody, just let off some steam. Put the gun down.' He became aware of the others in the saloon, men who'd retreated to the walls and the bartender edging towards the sawn-off by the till. 'Everyone take it easy,' he said, 'I'll handle this.'

'Handle it!' Freas said. It started as a snort and ended like a sob but in between Freas had started to lower and aim the six-gun in his right hand. Rhodes stepped quickly to his own right so that Freas would be shooting across his own body if it came to it.

It did. Whether Freas intended it or not the shot rang out, the big bullet ploughing harmlessly into the sanded floor.

But he had fired on a badge. Most lawmen would have gunned him down there and then, simply to survive, but moving to the left now Rhodes banged into an empty chair and reached instinctively to save it from falling. Almost as instinctively he swept it up and flung it at the drunk.

It was only a light cane chair but it caught Freas full in the legs. He reacted first by pulling the trigger again on the gun in his right hand.

Nothing: he'd emptied the cylinder.

He raised the gun in his left hand but the chair, while it hadn't knocked him down, had made him move too quickly and his balance was all wrong. He still didn't fall but swayed, needing both hands to restore his balance. The gun in his left hand went off, firing up into the ceiling.

Rhodes jumped at him, drawing as he did so, whether to shoot or not he never knew, for in a second they were tangled together and it was easier to coldcock him with the butt.

Freas went down like the proverbial sack of potatoes, the guns falling from his flaccid hands. Rhodes stepped back, gun still in hand, for an instant almost as ready to shoot as Freas had been. Then he was calm again. He reholstered the weapon and looked around.

'Anybody hurt?'

No one was, though the barkeep, who was also the owner, felt he was hurt financially and said so loudly.

Rhodes was unsympathetic. 'Sue him. Hell, you won't get any money but you'll make your own lawyer richer.'

The barkeep said nothing. He could see the logic of that. Rhodes felt like adding: why the hell did you keep plying him with cheap whiskey? But he didn't. He already knew the answer. For money. The same reason he tackled drunks in saloons.

'Kick the bastard!' someone shouted. Some deputies would. The damned fool had fired on the law, on a badge, and to some to let that go spelt anarchy.

Rhodes took a deep breath, bent, grabbed the drunken farmer by his belt and lifted him bodily.

'Leave him here, we'll see to . . . ' the barkeep began and stopped after one glance at Rhodes' face.

'God help anybody who makes any more trouble in here,' Rhodes said and walked out, pulling Freas after him, heels trailing across the sanded floor.

★　★　★

'Shoot him?' Sheriff Gilbey asked his chief deputy as he sprawled back, feet on the desk, in the county sheriff's office.

'I felt like doing.'

'You should have. It calms things down for a while.'

Rhodes said nothing, just half-dragged his bundle to the barred door that was the opening to the county jail and called out:

'Prisoner for you.'

A moment later Bisbee, the jailer, a tall cadaverous man, was there, opening up and looking down at his new guest.

'I heard the shooting. What's his name and what's the charge?'

'No charge, let him sleep it off and throw him out. His name's Toby Freas.'

'Where's his guns?' Bisbee asked, noting the empty holsters.

'They were on the floor in the Golden Slipper last time I saw them but the barkeep will have 'em by now. He'd be wiser to let him keep them.'

Bisbee bent swiftly, took his new charge neck and crop and carried him into the nether regions of his little world of dark, barred cells as if he were carrying a child. Rhodes stood there a moment, looking into the gloom.

'You're getting soft,' Gilbey said.

Rhodes turned, looked at him but said nothing. Gilbey hadn't got out of his chair when he heard the shooting but he had got himself elected county sheriff. Rhodes hadn't, hadn't even tried.

'Okay,' Gilbey said, 'I ain't got no complaints, just joshing.' He paused, then: 'Oh, there's a letter for you. On your desk.'

Rhodes walked over to the smaller desk, an open roll top set to one side of the office. He could see the letter in its brown manila envelope and wondered who'd be writing to him. There was an easy way to find out. He sat down, picked it up, examined the address. He didn't recognise the handwriting.

'Aren't you going to open it?' Gilbey was as impatient as a child sometimes. Rhodes considered sticking it in his pocket and telling Gilbey he'd read it later. That would irritate the hell out of him, but he found that for once he was impatient too. He tore open the envelope and read.

'Well,' Gilbey asked after he'd forced himself to wait half a minute, 'good news or bad?'

Rhodes was still of half a mind to tell Gilbey to go to hell, that it was his own private business, but Gilbey had picked the right question, the one he wasn't sure of the answer to himself. He said:

'Depends on how you look at it. It's bad — but it's good, too . . . '

PART ONE
THE TOWN

1

Rhodes glanced briefly at the sun. Another three hours till dark, he thought, and if he remembered aright he should just be riding into Gauntsville by then.

It had taken longer than he'd expected; the horse he'd hired in the livery in Sweetwater had seen better days, which was understandable — for all they had a reciprocal arrangement with the livery in Gauntsville it would still be out of circulation for three or four days and he was a passing stranger for all they knew. Why risk their best?

At last they came to the base of the butte that hid Gauntsville and Rhodes dismounted, tethered the animal and lit a cigarette. The final part of the trail was steep. They both might as well take a breather before attempting it.

He sat down on a rock, drew on the

handrolled cigarette and wondered again if he was doing the right thing. The lawyer's letter had said the horse ranch would fetch 1500 dollars. All he had to do was give his written permission in a letter and the money would immediately be wired to him.

That was a nice piece of change. He could have bought a part share in a saloon. Except he wasn't cut out to be a barkeep and certainly not a pimp which it often amounted to, nor even a silent partner to one. Ever since he'd got back from the war he'd been a law officer and an honest one.

He smiled to himself. There was precious little chance of getting rich wearing a star, not if you were honest and he was surely that. Almost painfully so he thought sometimes, but that was down to Uncle George who'd raised him — and left him his horse ranch. He'd never got rich from it but Uncle George had held his head high and the horses he sold didn't turn up lame a mile down the trail. Why not exchange fifty a month and a dollar fifty an arrest for a bit of honest work on his own land?

It was that which had really decided it. He'd never owned land before, just rented space in boarding-houses that called themselves hotels, and often enough bunked in the jail itself to save a few dollars a week. Having something of his own would be good.

He scrunched the cigarette out between his fingers and dropped the remains on the sparse grass of the trail.

'Time to get moving,' he said, either to himself or the horse, he wasn't sure which. It didn't matter: soon enough he'd be talking to horses unashamedly. Uncle George always had, claiming it was part of the breaking process.

The horse raised its head, somewhat dolefully, as if it knew what came next. It surely did: it had probably taken this trail a hundred times and knew the next part was the hard one, the one-in-three slope. Rhodes untethered it, started to mount up and stopped himself.

'Come on,' he said, 'I'll lead you up-slope. It'll be as quick.'

The horse just looked at him.

'Hell, another few years and I'll be hearing you answering back,' he said and laughed, recalling how Uncle George had been a lot more voluble with horseflesh than he ever was with humankind.

Whatever, horses did have one virtue, he thought as he led off: you never had to worry about them shooting you in the back.

2

Rhodes mounted up when they reached the crest and only then looked down on Gauntsville in the valley below. The town was shadowed from the low sun by the heights to the west of it and the lamps had already been lit, though he could still make out the shapes of the buildings — the livery, the various stores, the saloons and the Methodist church on the edge of it, its white-painted clap-board walls grey now in the shadow.

It hadn't changed much, if at all. But then why should it? Gauntsville had always been a backwater, servicing outlying ranches in the high country, with no chance of a spur line from the railroad and only very occasional stages arriving with lathered horses from the climb.

He set off down the trail, letting the

horse make its own pace. It would be stupid to risk a fall now in the failing light, and he found himself recalling his uncle's advice about riding at night — don't. But if you did, trust the horse.

Horses were about all that Uncle George had ever trusted. Certainly not Tom Rhodes. The hard old man never had a word of praise for him. Even when he'd told him he was enlisting all he'd got was a nod. But then he'd left him his ranch. The lawyer's letter had mentioned a will and the old man must have kept his rare letters for the address otherwise the lawyer would have had difficulty contacting him. Perhaps he should have come back after the war? Blood was blood.

He put the matter out of mind. It was past changing. The only thing he could do for him now was to run the ranch well . . . and try not to get too much like him.

★ ★ ★

Jimmy Tyson still had the livery. An old man then, now he was ancient with skin like a baked apple, and a stoop, but his eyes were keen.

'You're George Wilson's boy, ain't you?'

'His nephew.'

'A fine farrier, George,' the old man said, leading the horse to its stall, 'better'n any veterinarian I ever met, or am likely to.'

'Yeah,' Rhodes said, not really feeling like conversation with the spectre from the past. He wanted a soft bed and maybe a shot or two of whiskey before that but Jimmy Tyson would be one of his best customers. Besides, he wasn't about to deprive George Wilson of his due praise even if it were posthumous. Come to think of it, he'd got little enough of it alive. This was a hard, close-mouthed community.

'Come to settle up?' Jimmy said, looking over the horse. 'You didn't get her lathered up, I see. I'll leave her till morning, let her eat and rest. She's old bones, like me.' He paused. 'I'd have thought Old Miskeson in the Sweetwater livery would have done better by you.' He turned, looked Rhodes in the eye. 'Eh?'

'What?'

'You heard me. I asked if you'd come to settle up.' The old man looked almost fierce.

'No, I'm going to run the ranch myself,' Rhodes said, holding his temper. He too wasn't fond of giving out personal information, he realised, though there was nothing secret about that particular item.

'Humph,' the old man said after a moment. 'Get yourself killed if'n you want to, t'ain't no skin off my nose.'

'What do you mean? Rhodes asked quickly.

'Just what I said,' Tyson replied.

Rhodes didn't press him. If there was one thing there was no shortage of in any hick town, it was gossip. He'd know everything soon enough.

3

Lawyer Sandfort was dismissive of the old man's warning when Rhodes mentioned it to him the following morning.

'He's got strange over the years. Don't let it worry you.'

'So who wanted to buy the ranch?' Rhodes asked, studying the dark-suited man on the other side of the heavy desk, wondering why, as the only lawyer in town, he hadn't got himself made judge or justice of the peace.

'Er, well — '

'Who?'

Sandfort smiled. 'It's no secret, I suppose. The Sweetwater Cattle Combine put in an offer.'

'How much?'

'Eighteen hundred dollars.'

'Your letter said fifteen hundred.'

'I have my fees and your hired man to pay — '

'I have a hired man?'

'Somebody had to look to the horses. Jake Miles. Do you know him?'

Rhodes shook his head.

'No, you wouldn't, come to think of it,' Lawyer Sandfort said, scratching his balding head. He was a thin man with a narrow face and somewhat protuberant eyes. Rhodes had seen gamblers just like him. They usually cheated and got themselves caught at it, and shot too.

'No,' Sandfort continued, 'he drifted into the valley just a few years back. Your uncle was getting old, took him on to help out. Twenty a month and found. He's paid up to date. I've seen to it.'

'I'm obliged. Do I owe you anything for it?' Rhodes asked, expecting to be presented with a bill.

Lawyer Sandfort shook his head. 'Your uncle left a little cash too. I used it to pay his taxes to date and took my fee out of it but there's seventeen dollars still on account in the bank. I'll take you there and have it transferred into your name. I've already warned the teller to have the papers ready.'

'For today?' Rhodes asked. He'd only spoken to two people in town — Jimmy Tyson and his landlady. Whiskey had got itself put off the agenda somehow last night.

'No, when I got your wire. This mightn't be a big city like Abilene or Topeka, Mr Rhodes, but we're efficient enough, believe me.'

'I do,' Rhodes assured him, still a little surprised that he wasn't having to take out his wallet. Maybe he'd misjudged Sandfort.

'As for the ranch, I'll let you have an inventory. It's really just a list of numbers — I'm no judge of horseflesh, you understand — but it's pretty much as your uncle left it.' He paused, then: 'He was buried in his own plot on the ranch. The will — I'll let you have a copy of that too — specifically said he wanted no services. There was talk in town about that but I obeyed his instructions.' He paused again. 'It saved a little money.'

'Uncle George was never one for ceremonies,' Rhodes found himself saying, as if defending his uncle.

'His prerogative, sir, his prerogative. It's what we fought the war for — freedom of the individual! But I surely won't lecture *you* on that. You have a most distinguished war record, I recall, most distinguished.'

Rhodes shrugged slightly. Only civilians liked to keep bringing the war up. Those who'd suffered it preferred it forgotten.

Sandfort got to his feet. 'Shall we attend to business, sir?'

Rhodes stood up likewise. 'Yes, why not?' He paused. 'I'm obliged.'

Sandfort smiled. 'That's what we lawyers are for, sir. I'll get you your documents.'

As the lawyer busied himself at the filing cabinet Rhodes wondered again whether he hadn't misjudged him badly. All the same, if Sandfort were dealing cards he'd still watch his hands very carefully indeed.

4

Possessed of a bankbook recording a grand total of seventeen dollars and thirty-eight cents, now safely in his pocket, Rhodes set about exploring the town afresh. It hadn't changed much, just a few more stores and town houses than he remembered . . . and an extra saloon.

He wandered over to the church. A glance in through the window showed it was still doubling as a schoolhouse though the teacher was much younger than Miss Grice, who'd been a most formidable lady indeed. Her replacement was a hundred pounds lighter and quite pretty.

His uncle hadn't thought much of book work. A man needed to be able to read and write and cipher and that was enough, so Rhodes had found himself back on the ranch after completing eighth grade, learning instead the care of horses, especially cleaning out their stalls; sweeping the house out and cooking hadn't been neglected either.

Not that Uncle George had stinted himself when it came to work. It was a full section-sized ranch with access to free range in the east and there was never enough time. Unlike the city boys, Rhodes had found the army easy, almost a lazy life, until it came time to be shot at . . .

He retreated from the window, not wishing to be noticed, and glanced at the notice-board on the gate as he left. There was no mention of a specific minister. That wasn't unusual. Few stayed. The stipend was minuscule. The church had to depend on circuit-riding parsons for weddings and confirmations and some local old windbag most Sundays. Uncle George had mostly spared him that by not sparing him from the ranch.

He considered going across to the livery and trying his luck again with

Jimmy Tyson but soon thought better of it. He'd have more chance in a saloon when it came to gossip though he was beginning to doubt there was anything worthy of gossiping about in Gauntsville. So which of the three?

He doubted he'd be known in any of them — Uncle George hadn't approved of drinking nor of giving his nephew money to fritter away on anything. He eventually decided on the new one, the Grand Union, despite its name a clapboard construction of no vast size.

It was open but not unexpectedly empty at this hour of the morning. The barman was sweeping up after the night before but put down his broom to attend to his new customer.

'What'll it be?' he asked after hurrying behind the bar. 'Whiskey?' His hand was already reaching for the bottle.

Rhodes shook his head. 'I'll have a coffee if you've got a pot on.'

'Always,' the barkeep said and walked down to the other end of the bar. 'New in town?'

'You might say.' Rhodes paused. 'You too?'

The barman, a rotund little man of about thirty-five with receding red hair, smiled. 'I'm from Sweetwater. I came here last year.'

'Business that good, eh?'

The barman shrugged. 'I get paid either way. Here, at least, I'm my own boss most of the time.' He hurried back down the bar carrying a heavy blue-glazed cup brimming with black coffee.

Rhodes reached for his money.

'First drink's on the house, stranger.'

'I'm obliged.'

'Wait till you taste it.'

Rhodes blew on it, took a sip. It was steaming hot still but good coffee. He said as much.

'We aim to please,' the redhead said, smiling. 'My name's Frank Willis, by the way.'

'Thomas Rhodes,' he replied, taking the hand offered over the bar. Then: 'What's the set up in this town?'

'Much the same — '

'As when you left it,' a new voice said. Rhodes turned, almost spilling his coffee and saw a tall figure silhouetted in the doorway.

'Marshal Brand.'

'Chief Brand — as in Chief of Police. We try to keep up with the times.' The tall man sauntered across, then offered his hand too. 'Welcome back, Tom. I'm sorry about your uncle.'

'Thanks, but he was an old man, and by all accounts he went easy.'

'He didn't suffer,' Brand said. 'It was sudden, on the way to town.'

Rhodes wanted to ask for details but stopped himself. Why pretend he'd come back for anything but what he had — the ranch? For a long time now he'd barely thought about George Wilson, just enough to write him a letter once a year, if that.

'Can I buy you a drink?'

Brand shook his head. 'Too early for me and I get all the coffee I want from my own stove.' He paused. 'I hear tell you're planning on staying.'

Rhodes nodded. 'I thought I'd gather a little moss, see if I liked it for a change.'

'I heard you were marshalling down Kansas way.'

'Deputy was all, deputy sheriff. Collecting taxes and locking up drunks.'

'I don't do the first and try to avoid the last. They make one hell of a mess of your cells. Come to think of it, I don't know what they pay me for.'

'You're still here so they must know.'

'Unless it's pure habit,' Brand said, smiling. 'I see you're not carrying.'

Rhodes was suddenly aware of the empty space on his hip. 'I didn't think I needed it.'

'You don't,' Brand said. 'I only wish others felt the same. It's not the gunfighters I worry about — the wrong end of a sawn-off quiets them quickly enough — but some poor fool who couldn't hit a barn door with it sober. They give me the jitters every time.'

'So pass a city ordinance,' Rhodes said, knowing how hard it was to do.

The mayor and councilmen liked their hand artillery too.

'Maybe one day . . . '

'I'd drink to that if this was anything but coffee,' Rhodes said.

'Yeah. I'll be on my rounds now. I'll see you tonight?'

'No,' Rhodes said, 'I'm going straight to the ranch.'

'You've got a horse?'

'I thought I'd rent one from Jimmy.'

'Don't waste your money. My deputy has to be going that way today with the rig. I'll have him drop you off. Heck, we can't have horse ranchers renting horses!'

'Thanks.'

'No problem. Your saddle's at the livery?'

'Yeah, I'll — '

'No need. I'll tell Joe to get it for you. He'll be outside my office waiting in fifteen minutes. That do you?'

'Surely.'

'Least we can do for one of our own. Besides, I hear tell you did real well in the war. That reflects well on the town. Yes, sir! Welcome back, Tom.' And with that he left.

Rhodes stared down at the coffee. There was only one person Brand could have heard about his war service from — and Lawyer Sandfort too — and that was George Wilson. Had Uncle George boasted about how well his nephew had done?

He could scarcely credit it. But all the same, he knew it was so.

PART TWO
THE RANCH

1

Rhodes walked up the last rise of the off-trail that led to the ranch knowing exactly what he would see when he reached the top. Everything just as before. Except for George Wilson, who might have been proud of him at the last — and even all along? — but who had never showed it. He paused, hefted his saddle higher on his shoulder, took a grip on the saddle-roll under his arm and started off again.

Joe could have easily brought the rig up here but he'd stopped at the fork and grunted. An odd character, big as a house and yet with a faintly Mexican cast to his features, he hadn't spoken the whole ride. And where was he going on that trail anyhow? There was just miles and miles of flattish grazing land before you got anywhere. And what business had Brand — the *town* marshal — to send his deputy out there? But that was none of his business. Then he was over the rise and looking down at the ranch and . . .

Nothing had changed at all. It was as if the years had rolled back and he was looking down as he'd looked down that last morning on his way to town, on his way to enlist. Uncle George hadn't come out then, either.

He sighed. The years hadn't really rolled back: a boy had left, a man had arrived. All the same he gave a whoop and started running down the track in a flurry of dust and flying grit.

He stopped and caught his breath when he was at last on the level, staring at the unchanged ranch house, small and strongly built, the great barn and the corral beside it. And . . .

He slipped the saddle from his shoulder and let fall the saddle roll, walking over to the little enclosed space where the graves were, taking his hat off as he did so.

There were four graves now, his ma

and pa's, just names and dates with the same epitaph on both — *taken by the fever* — neatly carved in the now ageing wood. He'd never known them to recall. Nor his aunt, George's wife, whose shared grave was next — EMILY AND JOHN with the epitaph *died in childbed* — below it.

He stood a moment before each, wondering what to feel, as he always had, for people he'd never known, then moved on to the fourth and newest. It was just a name, GEORGE WILSON, and a date with no epitaph at all, neither had it been carved but burnt in with an iron by someone less than perfectly skilled in its use. Even the wood was roughly shaped.

No matter. Whether you were a pharaoh with a mountain of stone set over you or you got a shallow grave with no marker at all, you were just as dead. George would have agreed with that.

Rhodes turned suddenly and walked over to the house.

Jake Miles was waiting for him in the main room. He was a surprise. Rhodes had expected an oldish man but Miles was only in his thirties, quite presentable in his way; he'd shaved that morning and his hair was neatly combed. He was of average height, maybe a touch on the thin side but not scrawny. Yet there was something.

'I didn't come out,' Miles said. 'I thought you'd want your privacy.' His accent wasn't local and he sounded well educated.

Rhodes offered his hand. Miles took it, smiled slightly; not mockingly but, Rhodes suddenly realized, fearfully. Miles was terrified of him. Why?

'I've fed the horses,' Miles said. 'I've checked those out to pasture too. No problems there. The herd's doing well. The supplies need topping up though. Nothing's been replaced since George died.'

'Why not? Were you refused credit?'

'I didn't ask. I wasn't sure . . . ' He broke off.

And suddenly Rhodes understood. It fitted. Miles was a rummy. Not just a drunkard but a man totally addicted to the stuff. He'd seen them in all the towns he'd worked in, cadging drinks at the bars, often enough topping up that supply with their own vile concoctions, anything to get enough to keep going. Nobody arrested them, you fed them in jail and they vomited it back; if you didn't feed them, they vomited anyway for want of alcohol. And when they couldn't supplement their cadging with a bit of mucking-out work to get a few dollars for booze, they were going down fast. In winter you'd often find them frozen in the snow, stone dead.

Miles knew the look he was giving him. He said:

'I'll get my things together — '

'Hey, who said anything about leaving? Unless you want to.'

'No, sir!'

'If George Wilson kept you on, you

know your job. And I need help.'

Miles's relief was obvious. 'Thanks, I . . . ' He broke off again.

Did he really want a rummy working the ranch? Rhodes asked himself. But he'd really no choice. George had kept him on and besides, kicking him out would be pretty much like killing him. He shook his head in wonderment. He couldn't imagine George taking on a rummy but he indisputably had.

'What about the drink?'

'George got me down to half a pint a day. He watered it up to a pint. Since he died I've kept to the same.'

Which would have been hard. 'I'll do the same for you if you want, or you can do it for yourself, if you can. Okay?'

Miles nodded. He looked like a man who'd just been reprieved, which he had been.

'Look, I'll go get my saddle and roll and you can make up a cup of coffee, then you can tell me about the ranch.'

Outside, Rhodes took his time, knowing Miles would probably be weeping with relief. He rolled a cigarette and thought about things. So George had had a heart after all — and seemed to have willed it to him along with the ranch.

Hell, at least he'd have someone to talk to, aside from the horses.

2

Miles made more than coffee, he made a meal of eggs and bacon and fried pan-bread. Rhodes wolfed it down. 'So, tell me about the horses. Sandfort's list says there are thirty.'

'Yeah, in the corral, but there's another fifty on the range. Good stock, all of them. I can get the books . . . '

'Later,' Rhodes said, adding up the value of the ranch afresh. Sold even at their cheapest the horses were worth half as much again as he'd been offered and probably much more than that if they were good stock. Add in the land and the buildings and the price Sandfort had tried to get him to sell for was way, way too low. Something more like 5000 dollars or a substantial part of it was nearer the mark.

Well, Sandfort was a lawyer, after all, and he'd done the paperwork well enough, Rhodes thought. The land was now in his name, taxes paid and everything duly recorded. Probably Sandfort had helped himself to some change but aside from the seventeen dollars in the bank Rhodes had his own savings, just over 1000 dollars. He needn't beg for credit this year and if he sold horses he'd be in profit.

He questioned Miles further. George had sold to the livery stable, supplied the remudas of the little ranches to the north of Dodd's Peak, he learnt, and had usually taken two dozen horses a year down to Sweetwater. On impulse Rhodes asked if he'd sold anything to the Sweetwater Combine.

'No, never,' Miles said. 'The horses were for the livery there and private sales in town.' He paused. 'The Sweetwater Combine is just a name. They don't even have an office there. It's really a big outfit based on the old Casa Colorada ranch with a dozen of the big ranches to the east bought up too. They reckon they've a lien on all the grazing lands north of the Southern Buttes.'

That was new. There'd been no truly huge ranches when he'd left. He pressed Miles further and discovered there were still plenty of small ranches left around Dodd's Peak though the two horse ranches high up on it had failed. So what they'd lost in the east they'd gained in the west. The ranch was a going concern. He reckoned he could make a thousand dollars clear in a good year. He didn't say that to Miles though. You could trust a rummy only so far.

He stood up. 'Let's go and have a look at the horses.'

★   ★   ★

The horses were much better than he'd expected. George had bred the herd up in the intervening years. Of the thirty in the barn and corral twenty were already broken for riding and the other ten well on the way. Every one had a glossy coat and good teeth. They'd all fetch top price. They were probably the best of the herd but if the rest were even half as good, Lawyer Sandfort really had tried to cheat him.

'Let's check the grazing stock,' he said.

'I'll saddle up a pair of horses. Do you want to choose your own?'

'We'll take the rig,' Rhodes said. The ride from Sweetwater was nothing to what he'd done in the war but his 'riding calluses' had worn off in the meantime.

'You might care to take your gun,' Miles said.

'Why?'

'The Combine boys can be a touch awkward — at least, so I've heard tell.'

'On my land?'

'I haven't had any trouble,' Miles admitted.

Probably not. Miles would be as wary as a rabbit, like all rummies.

'How many riders do they have?'

'About two dozen. The ramrod is a

man called Manolito Cahane, Mexican-Irish, but nobody calls him a greaser. Not to his face.' He paused. 'He was the one who found your uncle on the road.'

Rhodes didn't reply, just nodded at the rig and let Miles harness up the horses. It was a while since he'd harnessed up a rig. He wondered whether he should wear his six-gun but in the end he didn't bother. There was already a loaded Greener 12-bore in the rig's gun sheath and that should be enough for safety. He hadn't come here to play gunfighter. He'd already done that for real.

* * *

The horses in the north of the section were as good if not better than those in the corral, not really a bad specimen amongst them. He noticed how good Miles was with them, how they'd come up to him.

'How safe is this pasture?' he asked

when Miles climbed back up.

'It's fine. There's been no wolves hereabouts in five years and the catamounts stay close to Dodd's Peak.'

'What about the human sort of pests?'

'We've had no trouble.'

'Not even with the Combine?'

'No.'

Well, if they intended to steal the place through a lawyer, why bother to steal physically? But he might be misjudging them. Whatever, this was good grazing. To bring the herd in at nights would be a last resort, not a first.

'Let's get back,' he said. 'I'd better see what stores we need.'

He let Miles drive. He did it well. Aside from being a rummy he seemed a good enough guy and Rhodes wondered about his background. It would be easy enough to find out. Miles had relaxed but there was still a touch of anxiety about him yet. He'd open up if asked. Except Rhodes knew he couldn't do that. A man had a right to his privacy, and his past.

'Breaking the horses in will be a problem. I'm out of practice. How are you?'

'I try,' Miles said. 'I can't say I'm very good.'

'So who did George get in to do it?'

Miles turned in his seat to look at him. 'Nobody. He did it himself, mostly.'

'But I got the impression he was . . . showing his age, that he fell out of his saddle.'

'I don't know. I wasn't there,' Miles said. 'But he'd been breaking horses the day before and he didn't fall off once, or even look like it. He was a tough old *hombre*, believe me.'

Rhodes did, and was rather sorry that he did. Maybe he was clutching at straws but there was something about the whole set-up that didn't sit well with him. Maybe it was just that he'd seen too much chicanery in his time as a deputy . . .

After a while he asked Miles about

the funeral, keeping it casual — who was there, what was said? Miles gave him a fair report; he even volunteered that the coffin had been closed, apparently without reading anything into it himself.

Rhodes was silent after that. He lit a cigarette and drew on it as they neared the ranch he'd inherited.

3

Manolito was angry. The quirt which usually dangled from his wrist was in his hand and tapping lightly on the seam of his trousers as he stood arrogantly before Lawyer Sandfort's desk.

Sandfort's eyes kept being drawn to it. Rumour had it that the quirt was loaded with lead and that Manolito preferred it as a weapon to the *pistola* — in effect, a custom-made shotgun with six-inch barrels — that he carried in a holster across his stomach.

'There was nothing I could do,' Sandfort said. 'I explained it to Mr Adies. The will was clear — '

'You could have lost it.'

'The ranch would still have gone to him eventually. Someone would have sent him a letter. He wasn't unknown around here. His exploits as a lawman — '

'So why didn't you buy it?'

'He didn't want to sell.'

'For fifteen hundred dollars?' Mano-lito almost snorted.

'It wasn't a bad offer. Plenty of horse ranches sell for less. If I'd offered him too much, he might have got suspicious. It was the right offer, just as I told Mr Adies — '

'Mr Adies isn't interested in excuses, Sandfort. Neither am I. You even paid his taxes on time!'

'I'd have gone to jail if I hadn't. There was money in the bank to pay them. There was no way not to — '

'There was no way to do this, no way to do that . . . ' He paused. 'The Combine employs men to *find* ways.'

'There's still time,' Sandfort said quickly. The insistent tapping of the quirt had got badly on his nerves. 'The bridge — '

'We'll not talk of that here!'

'As you say. But I could up the offer to three thousand dollars.'

The motion of the quirt ceased for

the second time as Manolito considered the matter. He was a striking man, just enough over average height to be called tall and regular featured enough to be called handsome, though he rarely was. His most obvious feature was the contrast between the sandy blond hair of his Irish ancestry and the ink-black eyes of his Mexican side.

He made a decision. 'No! It's too low anyway and a further offer would be suspicious. Mr Adies wants it all to go smoothly. Our . . . partners don't want reports in the newspapers or cases in court.'

Which was precisely the reason it should stay in my hands, not yours, Sandfort thought, but he didn't say it. He didn't want to start that quirt tapping again. Instead he said:

'We could always go back to just asking for the right of way.'

Manolito looked at him coldly. 'George Wilson wouldn't agree to it.'

'You didn't buy his horses. He was an old man, set in his ways. Rhodes might be more reasonable.'

Manolito just looked at him.

'We could offer him a thousand dollars for it,' Sandfort said quickly. 'He'd have to be mad to refuse. The trail's already there. He doesn't stop people using it now. A thousand dollars cash — '

The quirt slapped hard against Manolito's leg. 'Try it then, on your own responsibility. But you'd better be right!' And with that he turned and strode out of the office.

* * *

Sandfort let out his breath in a low whoosh. Manolito terrified him. With good reason. But Adies was, if anything, worse. Why the hell had he got himself involved with these people?

But the answer was obvious — money. It was a small town to support a lawyer, especially as they'd never made him the local magistrate. He'd had to scratch and claw for fees here and there until the Combine came along. And it had all seemed so simple . . .

Maybe it still was. A thousand dollars was a lot of money for a right of way that Rhodes would lose nothing by agreeing to. He could even hint the Combine might eventually buy horses from him — just so long as it wasn't down on paper, what did it matter? In a year the Combine would be everything, the rest nothing, and the Combine's lawyer would be a rich man.

He reached quickly down and opened the right-hand side drawer of his desk, brought out the half-full pint flask of whiskey. He didn't bother with a glass, just poured a slug of the anaesthetizing fluid straight into his quaking stomach.

It had the desired effect. Rationality returned to his office. And the world. Rhodes was a reasonable man. No reasonable man would refuse an offer like that. Rhodes would accept.

He still took another slug to make the syllogism more certain.

PART THREE
THE COMBINE

1

Rhodes sat uncomfortably in the saddle. He'd spent two hours that morning breaking horses. At seventeen he'd been good at it; now, it was something of a chore. And an ache. He'd get back into it but he couldn't help recalling that when he was chief deputy — in the morning, at least — he'd be sitting on the stoop of the county sheriff's office with a cup of coffee and a cigarette watching the world go by.

Or not. Often enough not: nothing could be so deserted as a Western town at the right hour, or so peaceful. And a peace officer desired nothing so much as peace. Shooting was fine for dime novels but there the hero never stopped a bullet and the villains were vulnerable to his six-gun at 200 yards, despite the fact that no one he ever knew could guarantee to hit a house at 200 yards.

Just about that distance away the herd were about their eternal business of grazing. City horses got fed grain but you couldn't afford to do that on a horse ranch where it was grass, grass and more grass. He was also trying not to think about that closed coffin. Despite everything it was hard for him to like his uncle but blood was blood and there was something very iffy about his death. Having Sandfort over yesterday trying to buy a right of way through his land on very generous terms had only added fuel to the fire.

And yet he knew not to look for crimes. People came to you with their complaints and you did something about them, but you never, ever, drummed up trade. That way led to insanity. And yet . . .

He changed his position in the saddle. It didn't do much good. Maybe the thing to do was to leave the herd, which looked to be in good order, and go back to his work at the corral. He couldn't leave it all to Miles just because he was good at it.

That had surprised him. You didn't expect a rummy to be much use at anything but he was good about a horse ranch. In fact, he'd yet to see Miles take a drink. He did, no doubt of that, but never in public. Nor ever showed himself the worse for it.

His mind switched back to that closed coffin and that tricksy lawyer's offer of yesterday. As for the first, there was one way to find out. With a shovel. But he had a prejudice against that. Besides, he just couldn't see George falling off his horse. Not if he were fit, and Miles said he was . . .

He was reaching for the makings when he saw the rig coming up the trail. A girl was driving it, a very pretty one in a green gingham dress with a blanket jacket thrown over it. Alice Sims, the schoolteacher. He remembered her from before he'd left now, all freckles and big teeth.

He set his horse to meet the rig,

walking slow. She slowed too.

'School's out?'

'The start of a week's holiday,' she said, drawing level. 'I'm going home.' She paused, then: 'I lodge in town weekdays. It's part of my salary, the town pays for it. But it's good to go home.'

'Yeah, you're right,' he said, noting that the freckles had all gone and her teeth were just the right size. 'I'll ride with you if I may.'

She smiled. 'You may indeed.' She pulled the horse to a stop. 'You can drive, if you want.'

'You mean I may drive if I wish,' he said, dismounting.

'I do indeed!' She laughed. 'The sheriff correcting the schoolteacher's grammar . . . '

'Horse rancher,' he corrected, tying his horse off and climbing aboard. 'A peace officer's life is mostly waiting about. Some drink, some read books.'

'And you read,' she said, handing over the reins.

He nodded. 'Thought of being a lawyer once but I decided I was too honest to make a success of it.'

'I wouldn't dare tell my pupils that!'

'They don't need telling,' he said, getting the rig in motion. 'They already know.'

She smiled. 'I remember you from before. I saw you in church . . . before the war.' She didn't add she'd also seen him at her window a few days back.

'With my hair slicked down and choking in a collar and cravat,' Rhodes said, remembering.

'You looked very handsome to me.'

'I'm obliged, ma'am.'

'Oh, don't call me that. I get enough of it every day in the school. They don't tell you at Normal School how old it makes you feel.'

Rhodes laughed. 'I wouldn't worry about that for a while, Alice — I may call you that?'

'May and can, Tom Rhodes!' she said and laughed with him.

2

Alice's father, Magnus, was Rhodes' nearest neighbour and a potential customer. He had three sons too, one in the army, and his cattle spread was the biggest of the small ranches in the Dodd's Peak area though not in the same class as the Combine. George Wilson's ranch had always supplied him with horses and as a boy Rhodes had ridden this trail many times, but never so pleasantly.

Alice was three years back from Normal School in the state capital and had no particular beau. Rhodes got the impression that she worried that her education put them off and she'd end up an old maid. Needlessly, he thought.

'You surprise me, Tom,' she said suddenly, 'not wearing a gun. Everybody else round here seems to. Even on Sundays half the men wear them coming and going, only to hang them up on pegs in the church vestry.'

Rhodes found he rather liked being called Tom by her. It was years since he'd been anything but Rhodes. She used the name as easily as if he'd scarcely been away any time. And why not? He'd been part of her childhood here and what was more natural than that he was back?

'You get weary of guns,' he said. 'As a peace officer you carry one but it's just a tool of the trade. It's not like a cowboy wearing one to pretend he's something else — a gunfighter. Most of them are anything but.'

'I know. I'm a better shot than any of my brothers.'

'Then I'll let you have my gun. You can wear it to church on Sundays.'

Alice laughed like a schoolgirl rather than a schoolmarm and Rhodes was sorry that the Sims ranch had just hove into sight.

* * *

Magnus Sims was a bear of a man but a jovial one. He immediately took Rhodes into his best room and plied him with quite decent whiskey out of a jug. Rhodes didn't try to keep up with a host who looked as if he could down the whole jug without showing any ill effects whatsoever.

'I'm glad you're back, Rhodes, though I'm sorry for your loss,' Sims said. 'Pity you didn't come back straight after the war but I understand. George Wilson was a good man in his way but hard to live with, I bet.'

Rhodes just nodded. He liked Magnus Sims but felt no inclination to discuss family matters with him. Magnus didn't notice his reticence. The soul of tactlessness, he never did.

'I hear tell you ain't married. That makes you a catch in the valley — a man of property, a rancher, and probably with a few dollars put aside, eh?'

'I came back to ranch — ' Rhodes began.

'A rancher needs to be a family man. Look at me, three sons and a pretty daughter. Come to think of it, you'd make a good match for her. You ain't old but you're no kid any more and with all this school business Alice is getting no younger. My wife was fifteen when I married her and me not much older and that's the right age, believe me.'

Rhodes nodded again — a gesture, any gesture, was safer than words. Magnus poured himself another drink.

'You'd better not tell Alice I said anything — she gets upset, says I'm trying to marry her off.' He laughed. 'Hell, I reckon I am at that!'

Rhodes smiled politely. 'So how's business, sir? Any trouble with the Combine?'

'They push, but with the horse ranches on Dodd's Peak packed in, there's grazing enough. So I needn't push back.'

Rhodes told him about the offer he'd had from the Combine for the right of way.

'A thousand dollars just for a right of way! Hell, that's quite an offer. I'm surprised you didn't take it.'

'I've just been back a few days. I'm keeping my options open.'

'Cain't gainsay that none,' Magnus said. 'A sensible man does keep his options open. Another drink?'

'I'm fine. In fact, I'd better be getting back.'

'And not met my boys. Derry, my eldest — you remember Derry?'

'Yes,' Rhodes said, and he did; as a kid he'd been the spit and image of his old man, except where Magnus was jovial Derry was deadly serious.

'My youngest, Sean, he's still a schoolboy but he's a good kid even if I say so myself.'

'He's still in town?'

'Hell no, out with Derry.' Magnus scratched his head, then: 'Oh, I see. Why wasn't he with his sister? That's because he's got his own pony. It's hard enough being the schoolmarm's brother . . . '

'All the same, two's safer than one riding over this country. Rhodes said, surprising himself. It was none of his business. He got to his feet. 'I'll be seeing you, sir. Maybe sell you some horses.'

'Count on it!'

Alice came out as he was unhitching his horse.

'I just wanted to thank you for the escort.'

'My pleasure.'

'In which case, I shared it,' Alice said. 'Will I see you at church on Sunday?' she asked.

Rhodes had had no intention of going to church that Sunday or any other.

'Barring accidents, you can count on it,' he said.

★ ★ ★

That evening Rhodes brought the conversation round to Alice.

'She's a real lady,' Miles said simply.

Rhodes left it at that, a little ashamed of himself for even asking. Not that he really had asked anything, he told himself quickly.

'I think I'll go into town this Sunday. You can manage?'

'Sure,' Miles said, adding: 'I'm not much of a churchgoer myself but it lets you meet people.'

'You're right,' Rhodes said. And there was no reason why he couldn't have a word with Brand about George Wilson's death, kill two birds with one stone.

Maybe he was chasing shadows but there was something about the set-up around Gauntsville that set his teeth on edge. Brand had to be the man who knew all the answers.

He lit a cigarette and found himself not thinking of Brand at all but of a girl in a gingham dress . . .

3

As it turned out, there was no need to drive to town to see Brand; he turned up of his own accord. Miles had already seen him and made himself scarce, out of habit, and Rhodes took him into the main room where Brand accepted a cup of coffee.

'It's about the right of way, isn't it?' Rhodes asked.

Brand nodded. 'I'd take it as a personal favour if you'd accept. It's on the level.'

'I don't recall that I owe you any favours,' Rhodes said.

'Then do yourself a favour and take the money,' Brand said with sudden conviction.

'Before I do anything I want to know why my uncle was buried in a closed coffin.'

Brand suddenly looked very old.

'Well?' Rhodes pressed him.

'His head was stove in. It could have been caused by a fall.'

'But you didn't believe it.'

'You've heard of Manolito Cahane?'

Rhodes nodded.

'He carries a loaded quirt. It could have been that.'

'So why didn't you arrest him?'

Brand stared down into his coffee cup.

'Were you afraid to?' Rhodes went on remorselessly.

'Yeah, you might say I was.'

Rhodes studied him. Brand had been past his best even before he'd left, a man living on his reputation. Not much money but free drinks, lodging and meals found by the townsfolk who wanted a man with a star there so they could sleep nights. They usually got what they paid for — burnt-out cases. But Brand had been more; his nerves hadn't gone, he'd just been getting old.

'They own you,' Rhodes said coldly.

Brand looked up at him. 'God help

you if you end up old and poor! Beside, it wasn't like that. They paid for a deputy, said they wanted law and order. Hell, you could see I didn't need a deputy. And maybe I got a little to set aside for my old age, but I wasn't so different from the rest. How many drinks did you pay for when you were wearing a star?'

'We're not talking about drinks.'

'No, we're talking about George Wilson.' He paused, then: 'I reckon you're right. Manolito did kill him, but I couldn't prove it then and you can't now. Old men do fall off horses.'

'Why did they kill him?'

'For what they've asked you for, a right of way. George wouldn't give them one so they offered good money for the ranch. He wouldn't sell that either.'

'And so he had to die.'

'I had nothing to do with it!' Brand protested. 'And afterwards there was nothing I could do. It's not just the Combine, there's railroad money

69

behind it too. It's a juggernaut, Rhodes. Stand in its way and it'll crush you. Take the money. Sandfort says they'll give you the thousand for the right of way and he thinks he can get four thousand for the ranch too. Take it. Hell, you always hated George. He was a cold, hard man.'

'But he was my blood.'

'Your own will be no use to you spilt.' Brand sighed. 'I'll tell you everything. The idea is to build a spur line up from Sweetwater. That way the Combine can ship eight thousand head a year.'

'Over the butte? It's impossible, the gradient's way too steep.'

'True, but it's feasible if you run it skirting the butte, up through South Butte Pass and then build a bridge at the far end of the valley.' He paused. 'There's that much money in it.'

'But everything's useless to them without the trail through my land. It blocks the passage from the north into town.'

Brand nodded. 'Now do you see how

important it is?'

Rhodes ignored the question. 'Does the rest of the town know?'

Brand shook his head. 'They just think the Combine's thinking of moving its HQ into town, that's all.'

That made sense. Why push up land prices when you're buying?

'So you'll agree?' Brand asked.

'If they'd offered me five thousand dollars a bit earlier, I would have accepted for sure. But now I know they killed my uncle. Maybe I didn't like him but he raised me. He didn't have to. I reckon that I owe him something.'

'Not getting yourself killed. Twenty men ride behind Manolito Cahane and he's just the ramrod. Mr Adies at Casa Colorada has railroad money behind him. You can't win.'

'I don't need to win, Brand. I just need to stay here. If they push, I'll talk. I know this about spur lines — they cost big money. You have to make a good case for them. If there's a problem

71

or bad publicity, there's always some-where else.'

Brand stood up, shaking his head. 'I did my best.'

'There's a grave outside. Go and tell that to George Wilson.'

'You're as crazy as he was!'

'Maybe.' Rhodes paused, then: 'Don't come here again.'

Brand turned and left.

★　★　★

Maybe he's right, Rhodes thought. And maybe he'd been too hard on the old man. He put the matter aside: Brand had sold his badge. It mightn't have been much of one, chief of police of a village that called itself a city, but he'd never done that himself. Not once. And he wasn't about to change, whether he was wearing a badge or not, so he'd have to live with the consequences. Or die with them.

He heard Brand moving off and went to the door, watched him go up the rise and over it. He ran to it himself, keeping low when he got to the top.

Brand wasn't riding west, to town. He was riding east.

To the Casa Colorada.

4

Chief Brand was uneasy. He didn't particularly care for Manolito as a fellow-rider but Mr Adies had sent him along and there was no avoiding it. Manolito himself didn't terrify him. Men with sombreros and *pistolas* never had, nor any kind of common thing. Manolito was just a tool — Mr Adies was the will behind him. And, he admitted to himself, he was afraid of *him*.

The man had power; it almost exuded from him; it had been hard standing in front of his desk admitting failure. Mr Adies's eyes had seemed to bore into him as if he'd realized that Brand had admitted everything to Rhodes. Of course he'd said nothing of that; George Wilson's death hadn't been mentioned, had never been mentioned. Mr Adies didn't worry over details, just results. But he demanded them.

'I don't like men who hide behind badges,' Manolito said suddenly, bringing Brand's mind instantly back to the present.

'Why?' he said, turning to look at Manolito only to find he had dropped back a length. And that the *pistola* was no longer in its holster. It was pointing at him.

'Hey, Mr Adies won't like — '

'But he will. He told me before we left. 'That marshal sweats too much,' he said.' Manolito laughed. 'And you did.'

'He didn't mean for you to kill me,' Brand said quickly, looking into the dark eyes. 'Hell, I'm on your side. I'm still of use. I've got a legal gun.'

'But the law has failed us, you and Sandfort alike. It's time for my war now.'

Something in the eyes told Brand what was coming. His hand moved towards his gun but too slowly. Yet even had he been twenty years younger he couldn't have beaten a levelled gun. No one could.

He heard it roar and felt the impact in the same instant. There was no pain. Manolito had aimed to finish him with one shot, he realized — and had.

He thought: I should have — And then he was falling into blackness.

Taking extra care not to get blood on his clothes, Manolito set the dead marshal belly down over the saddle of his horse. Fortunately the shooting hadn't spooked it at all. But a marshal's horse — even one who called himself 'chief of police' — was used to gunfire.

He would have preferred to kill him with his hands but Adies had said to shoot him, so he had. Adies was not a man to cross even though he'd never see the body. And nor would anyone else. There were places in the Southern Buttes where you could lose horse and rider for ever, and he would.

Brand didn't need tying down, he decided. His dead weight would keep him atop the horse by itself unless they went at a gallop, and there was no hurry at all.

He glanced round at the grassland about him — not even a solitary cow in sight. He had picked his place well. It would seem as if Brand had just fallen off the face of the earth. Exactly as Adies wanted. He smiled, the dark eyes taking on a cold kind of life for once. The soft times were over. A phrase of his mother's language came to mind — *era la hora de la sangre*.

It was the hour of blood.

And it was just beginning.

PART FOUR
MANOLITO

1

'Easy boy,' Rhodes said, rubbing a white-flashed nose, 'I'm the fella that gives you your oats and currycombs you. You can trust me.'

It worked. Probably not the sentiment, Rhodes judged, but the tone. He was trying a technique he had seen his uncle use, Indian-gentling the horse. The trick was to get so you could touch any part of the horse without troubling it — to give it absolute trust in you. It took fair words and much patience.

Odd how George Wilson had been so good at it, being remarkably short of fair words for people. Whatever, it was easier on the backbone than the sheer brute force of breaking a horse rodeo style.

In the end he'd have to mount up and there might be some bucking but, if it worked, it should be of a different order. Or so he hoped. He started patting the horse's neck gently, and then caught sight of Miles at the barn door.

There was something different about him . . . and then he realized: he was wearing a gun. As Miles approached Rhodes could see it was the old Dragoon Colt in his uncle's old holster, the one he'd made for himself.

Miles noticed his glance. 'I borrowed it,' he said, 'after I saw you'd taken to wearing your gun again.'

Rhodes was briefly aware of the comforting weight on his right hip. 'Heck, you can have it. I doubt it's worth much anyway. It's not been converted to cartridges.'

'I'm used to cap-and-ball revolvers,' Miles said. He half-smiled: 'If six shots don't do it, it's never going to get done anyway.'

'You don't know who you're taking on,' Rhodes said.

'I'm afraid I do. When Brand spilled the beans I was in the bedroom . . . '

He looked down at his feet.

Rhodes wasn't annoyed. More amused. Miles was a queer sort of rummy indeed. They were usually petrified of guns. He patted his horse on the neck again.

'Remember who your friend is,' he instructed it, then to Miles: 'Let's go to the house. We need to talk.'

★   ★   ★

Inside, Miles started to take off the gunbelt.

'Leave it on,' Rhodes said, pouring coffee for both of them. 'As I said, it's yours.' He sat down, nodded for Miles to do the same. 'Now, I want to know why you're so willing to fight.'

'Whether you can trust a drunk?' Miles said without bitterness.

'I'm not judging you, Miles. It'd be too easy. Drink's no temptation to me. George Wilson was a teetotaller and while I'm not quite that, I soon could be.' He took out the makings. 'Cigarette?'

'No thanks, I never got the habit.'

Rhodes poured the fine, dry tobacco

into the paper, thinking about the word. Drinking and smoking were both just habits. You could break yourself of either, or both. He said:

'To tell the truth, I can't see why George took you on. He was — '

'Kind to me,' Miles said. 'It was three years ago. I asked him for the price of a drink. He asked my name, looked me over and then asked if I wanted a job.' He paused, then: 'He knew what I was and he didn't try to make me stop. He rationed me, I told you. I'd be dead now if it hadn't been for him.'

Rhodes lit his cigarette with a lucifer. 'And that's why you want to fight, to pay him back?'

'No, I can't pay him back. He's dead. But you kept me on. I live here. You fight for where you live. I was taught that.' He shook his head. 'It's about time I remembered it.'

Rhodes was silent a moment, then: 'You might as well tell me.'

★ ★ ★

Miles was no storyteller, least of all about that, but it had been festering inside for long enough and he was grateful for the opportunity to get it out.

He had been in the war, a Confederate because his state was, an officer because his family had land and connections, and for a while it had gone well enough. He'd made captain, more out of influence than merit, but the men had liked him and he'd reciprocated. Eventually, after much guard duty and the odd skirmish, they'd had their first battle.

'Stanefield, Virginia. Did you hear of it?'

'No.'

'Well, it wasn't a very big one. A brigade affair. I was in command of a troop of horse ordered to take the Union guns. There was only one reinforced battery but they were a thousand yards off.

'It wasn't so bad at first. They were firing cannon-shot and falling short as they tried to get our range. Then we were close. They started firing grape-shot.

'Suddenly they were cutting us to pieces. I pulled my troop back.' He shook his head. 'God knows, I wish I hadn't. The general was all for court-martialling me but my colonel knew my family well. I was transferred instead, to the QM staff. Everybody knew why. That's when I started to drink.

'After the war I didn't go home. I decided to start afresh in the West. I gambled for a living. I was lucky for a while but drinking and gambling don't mix. You know the rest.' He looked straight at Rhodes, challeng-ingly. 'Maybe you don't care to fight with a coward at your side. Maybe I'll run again, I can't be sure.'

'You'd be right, if you really were a coward.'

'Believe me, I've ample proof.'

'No, you were told it and you believed it. Hell, you don't charge guns at that range. You saved lives. If the

Confederate Army was like enough to the Union Army that brigadier of yours would have ruined himself court-martialling you. Which is probably the real reason he didn't.'

'That's kind,' Miles said shortly.

'It's also true. Hell, I've seen real cowardice and listened to it too . . . ' He paused, then: 'You didn't make excuses for yourself. It would have been easy enough but you didn't. The truth is, you just got a bad break.'

Miles shrugged. 'Even if you're right, that's a long time ago. Ever since then I've been getting my courage out of bottles. Maybe I would run.'

'No, you wouldn't and you know it. Now you've got a second chance you're more likely to get yourself killed foolishly than run.' Rhodes paused. 'Heck, I shouldn't take you up on it. You heard Brand — I'm being a damned fool. I shouldn't let you risk yourself for me, but I will, and gratefully.'

Miles suddenly stood up. 'I'm obliged, sir.' Then: 'I'll see to the horses now.'

Rhodes sat there for a while, thinking. He hadn't lied to Miles but as to whether he'd stand fast, who knew with anybody? What still puzzled him was why his uncle had taken pity on a rummy. It just wasn't in character. And it didn't matter at all.

Or maybe it did. Had Uncle George taken Miles on as a substitute for his missing nephew? And why should I care if he had? Rhodes thought. He had the ranch from him but at seventeen he'd been glad enough to get away, and stay away.

Even now he wasn't defying the Combine out of love for his uncle, more out of sheer bloody-mindedness.

And then it struck him. George Wilson had asked Miles his name. Unexpectedly. How would a fundamentally rather courtly man like Miles answer a much older man? Not Jake Miles of the saloon. He'd say John Miles.

John.

It said it outside on the grave marker and it was in the family Bible. The child his aunt had borne and which had survived an hour had been called John. Had he lived, the boy would have been about Miles's age.

It was a pared-down bit of reasoning but it convinced Rhodes. Uncle George had never loved him; he'd even resented him. But blood was blood.

Rhodes tapped the gun on his hip. The chances were he'd pay his uncle back in kind. Without affection. Because blood was blood and it was the right thing to do anyway.

He looked around the room he'd shared with the old man for so long . . . so very long ago.

''We're a true pair,' he said softly. 'Cold-hearted bastards both.'

2

Alice Sims took the dress down from the hanger, then another and another until all were spread out on the bed. The green gingham he'd already seen and, aside from the colour, the blue gingham was just the same though it did bring out the colour of her eyes. But those were really for school anyway. Her dark 'going to church' dress was quite stylish but . . . dark. That left the dark orange and the plain blue.

Five good dresses had seemed enough a few days ago but no longer. She really needed to look her best now. It would have to be the plain blue. It was a rather bright blue and her parents would look askance but she wasn't about to wear the usual dark dress for church that Sunday, not for anything.

She glanced back at her home-carpentered wardrobe, its door open and only the mortar board and gown of her graduation from Normal School left. Both were a rich brown — the young men had had black alpaca but the girls had theirs coloured. The gown would make a good skirt, she thought. If she left school. She wore it on the first day of term only and it was rather a waste of usable material.

She recalled how he had looked in at the school window. She hadn't recognized him then as the boy who had gone away to war and turned into a hero. She'd been quite small at the time but she could still recall how handsome he'd been then, and if anything he was more handsome now.

The plain blue dress. She left it on the bed and started putting the others away. When she'd done she picked it up and went to the window to examine it in the light. It was perfectly good.

What are you wearing that for? her mother would say. *Setting your cap for some boy?*

Well, the truth was — yes. Except he

was a man, not a boy, a very fitting man indeed. Maybe he was a dozen years older but that too was fitting, not like the Thelma Giggs they'd talked about at Normal School who'd ended up marrying one of her own pupils — him sixteen and she twenty-four. How they'd giggled at that.

She smoothed down the blue dress and hung it up carefully. Then, on impulse, she took the dark dress down again and threw it on the floor. Now she could say it was dirty, that's why she wasn't wearing it. It was best not to be to obvious otherwise her brothers would only tease her, Derry in his slow, ponderous way and Sean . . .

Besides, there was all the difference in the world between a girl setting her cap at a man and getting him.

And yet he liked her. She'd felt that. And she was sure he hadn't intended to go to church until she'd suggested it. She smiled, recalling that he'd hardly hesitated at all.

Alice flung herself on the bed and

hugged herself as if she were sixteen again and she were in love. And realized she was. For all the briefness of her time with him it had happened. To her. And how did he feel?

She smile confidently. She would see him at church, probably his first visit in years . . .

3

Sean Sims clutched his wool jacket to him and imagined what it would be like in the saloons of Gauntsville tonight — Saturday night. Imagination was all he could manage as he'd never been in a saloon except in daytime, with his father, and only the last time had he been allowed a small beer — which he'd pretended to like but hadn't — but the word 'saloon' still conjured up in his mind a glamorous picture of gaiety, mellow whiskey and loose but lovely women, for all that he knew Gauntsville could boast just two weary drabs of no allure whatsoever. He completed the picture with a six-gun strapped to his leg and fancy spurs strapped to his heels. It took a little of the coldness of the evening away.

He could have been at home in the warm, watching his father read his paper and Derry his account books, but he'd volunteered anyway. A calf had been found half-devoured on the edge of Dodd's Peak. It could have just been a weakling but his brother Derry thought it might be the work of a catamount and so here he was with his old .30 calibre rifle — though no six-gun — watching.

He'd be warmer walking, he decided, and dismounted, tying his horse up to a stunted bush. Anyway he'd been given strict instructions not to ride anywhere on the peak itself and he knew it was very good advice. It was full of potholes and tiny crevices that made it dangerous enough in full daylight.

He left his horse and wandered northwards towards where they'd found the carcass. There was a rock thirty yards off from it which would make good cover.

He walked slowly, suddenly feeling very grown up with a gun over his arm, his pockets full of cartridges and out hunting alone. This was a man's job after all, not a schoolboy's, and next year he'd be finished with school anyway. His mother would have preferred him to stay on, maybe even go to college, but his father had agreed with him. He was to be a rancher, not a lawyer, and while he could read and cipher well enough he knew he just wasn't cut out for anything academic. Not like Alice.

He smiled. It was embarrassing for both of them, her being the schoolmarm. Though maybe worse for her. He was too big to be bullied and he not only loved his sister, he liked her too. She favoured everyone equally and was utterly without malice.

He reached the rock and saw the carcass. He looked around. It was near to where the ground began to rise sharply and to his left there were bushes and a couple of badly stunted trees — and shadows. He decided to have a second glance at the carcass. If it was more mangled than before the catamount must have already been back and would be unlikely to come again. He went over and studied it. It was exactly as before. He smiled to himself. Tonight he might well bag himself a catamount.

If he did, he decided, he'd skin it and give the fur to Alice to top a coat. Ma already had one like that. He went back over to the rock and settled himself down, watching and listening and occasionally diverting himself with images of the bright, exotic nightlife of Gauntsville and himself in the very centre of it. But even that got boring after a while and, leaning against the rock with his rifle leaning on it, he fell asleep.

$$\star \quad \star \quad \star$$

He awoke with a start. Somebody was kicking him. It was getting on for full dark but the moon was up and he could see them clearly — Manolito, Joe the Deputy and another rider, a weasel-faced man. It was the last who was kicking him from horseback.

'Wake up, kid. I'm speaking to you.'

'I'm no kid — and stop kicking me!' Sean snapped, getting to his feet.

'You've annoyed him,' Manolito said joshingly. 'Be careful, he's got a gun. A tough *hombre* like that might even use it on you.'

Weasel-face dismounted. 'You wouldn't do that, kid, would you?'

Without thinking Sean swung the gun barrel in his direction only to have it wrenched from his grasp. Weasel-face was quick.

'Don't do that, kid, it ain't healthy.'

'I don't think he's a kid at all,' Manolito said. He too had dismounted and was standing by the carcass. 'I think he's a thief who's been out killing stock.'

'It's Sims stock and I didn't kill it.'

'It looks like Combine stock to me. I can't see no Sims brand.'

'It's just a calf.'

Manolito started to walk over, leading his horse. 'One calf or a hundred head, it's all rustling. The Combine doesn't like rustlers.' He smiled, his teeth very white in the moonlight. 'The Combine always hangs rustlers.'

Suddenly Sean was deathly afraid. Before, Manolito had never been a threat to him — a kid, he was beneath his notice — but he had still heard the tales.

'Hell, what to?' Weasel-face asked. 'He ain't big but them trees are too damn low.' He paused reflectively, then: 'We could always dry-gulch him, I reckon.

'I didn't do nothing, mister,' Sean heard himself say. 'It was a catamount.'

Manolito laughed, ignoring him. 'You're right, *amigo mio*, they are too low. And dry-hanging takes too long.'

'We could always shoot him.'

'No, you should always make an example of rustlers. Tie him to the tree, facing it. But take off his jacket first.'

'I . . . ' Sean began but Weasel-face was already pulling him along and ripping his jacket off at the same time. Sean tried to fight back but he had only a boy's strength still and Weasel-face was strong.

His face was pressed up against a tree, his hands pulled round the trunk and tied off with a thong. Suddenly he felt very cold but somehow relieved too. At least they weren't going to hang him, probably just leave him here for the night. That frightened him too but much less. He could put up with the cold and —

Crack!

For an instant Sean wondered what it was and then he realized. A moment later it cracked again and this time in earnest, snaking out to touch his back. A bullwhip, he thought, and then the pain hit him like a charging steer. He bit into the tree bark, tore at his wrists as he tried to free himself.

Crack! And the pain was worse. It didn't seem possible but it was and maybe he screamed. He didn't know or care. This was worse than hanging.

Crack!

And this time he could hear himself screaming, through a mouthful of bark, and the scream got higher and higher as the bullwhip cracked again and again, turning him around the tree by its force — but that gave him no respite. Manolito was good with the whip, hitting the same spot every time.

And then it stopped. Manolito said something and then laughed. He mounted up then and Weasel-face too and they rode off in the direction of Gauntsville, its three saloons, two trollops, whiskey, bright lights and all. Oddly, what stuck in Sean's mind was that Joe the Deputy had never dismounted nor said a word through it all. What that mattered, he couldn't think.

Sean hung there in pain and silence. He still wanted to scream but his throat was too raw and he'd no breath. He felt like he was in a fire and burning. It seemed impossible he could feel so much agony and stay conscious, even stay alive. Maybe he could stop it, choke himself with bark . . . but the trunk was bare of it where he was.

'Oh God, let me die!' he thought, 'let the pain stop.'

Then he fell into the dark.

PART FIVE
THE VACANT STAR

1

Rhodes felt cheated. He'd had to put up with a lay sermon from Jim Olson, who was also the mayor and the owner of the general store — and on, of all things, cupidity! Today Olson had been all for treasures in heaven but tomorrow that would cut no ice; dollars would be required, on the barrel.

Afterwards, Rhodes had been clustered about by people welcoming him back and had had to pretend that he remembered little Johnnie and Jilly who had been in diapers when he'd left. It hadn't been exactly what he'd come for.

So where were Alice and family? Others had noticed their absence, which was apparently a rarity, but the general consensus had been that it would be one that would only be explained next Sunday.

Not with him there, he decided as he

sat in the Gauntsville Hotel bar with a
whiskey and a cigar and watched Jim
Olson at the corner table dealing poker
hands to his friends. He considered
going over to join them. He didn't
doubt for a moment that new money
would be more than welcome and he
usually did quite well at cards, playing
the odds rather than trying to bluff his
opponents. And he always knew when
to stop. Rather like Uncle George . . .

But he wouldn't play today. He'd felt
a little guilty leaving Miles on his own,
even with that ancient piece of hand-
artillery. For seeing Alice, he could
justify it. For gambling, no.

'Refill?'

Rhodes glanced down at his glass,
still half-full of liquor.

'No, but I'll take a dollar's worth of
cigars.'

The barkeep turned to count out the
cheroots and Rhodes emptied his glass.
He'd paid for it, he'd drink it. Then he
counted out ten dimes and set them on
the bar.

'One dollar precisely,' he said.

The barkeep handed him the cigars which Rhodes carefully slipped into his breast pocket, one by one. Cigars had been a real luxury during the war and he'd learnt to be careful with them. The habit had stuck.

'I wonder what happened to the Sims,' he said when the last one was safely ensconced.

The barkeep shrugged. 'That's church stuff. I just keep bar.'

Rhodes stood up and then sauntered over to the swing-doors. He'd better be getting back. And then he saw the wagon coming slowly down Main Street, Magnus Sims driving, his wife beside him and Alice in the back. Magnus's face was like a stone.

Out of long experience Rhodes just stood there, silent, and watched, drawing on his cheroot as he did so. The wagon passed the saloon and he could see Alice was kneeling over someone lying in the back. One of her brothers, he guessed. He couldn't see which.

Accident? Or something else? His first thought was pure relief that it wasn't her. Then he dropped the remains of his cigar and crushed it out underfoot. A moment later he set off after them.

2

Doc Gabriel was out, apparently attending a birth on the other side of Dodd's Peak. Rhodes remembered from before, a fumble-handed man of no great skill but with a good bedside manner. The latter was probably little diminished and the former little improved but he still wished he were there. The boy's back had been cut to ribbons.

'Manolito did it,' Magnus told him, 'Sean could still speak when we got to him — just.'

Who else? Rhodes thought, aware that everyone was looking to him. There was nothing for it but to do his best. He had them put the boy face down on the bed in the doctor's office and considered a moment. Then:

'Fetch me two bottles of whiskey.'

While he was waiting he cut away the shirt except on the back and took the opportunity to look his patient over more carefully. The wrists were bruised but aside from the back, that was all. Still, Sean was deathly pale and breathing shallowly. That was shock.

'His mouth was full of bark,' Magnus said. 'I cleaned it out.'

Rhodes said nothing. Then the whiskey arrived and he took the first bottle, poured half of it over the mess of blood and torn shirt, then slowly stripped it off. Sean groaned. Leaving the shirt on had been no kindness. Fragments of fabric in the wound would cause suppuration. He had to get them all. When he was sure he had, he emptied the rest of the bottle over the torn, naked back.

It brought Sean back to consciousness in an instant. He screamed.

'Get him on his side,' Rhodes ordered and they did, enough so for him to pour a good slug from the second bottle into his mouth. He lost most but enough went down.

'Scream all you want,' he told the

boy, 'but fight! You'll survive if you fight. Do you understand?'

The eyes seemed to say yes.

Rhodes turned away. 'That's it, there's nothing more to be done till the doc gets back. Give him all the whiskey he wants to start with — but no laudanum. He's better conscious than not.'

Magnus took him aside. 'Will he live?'

'If he wants to bad enough. The wounds are superficial and he hasn't lost too much blood. It's the shock. In the war you'd see some men just slip away with flesh wounds while others could lose a limb and live.'

'Why?' Magnus asked and Rhodes realized he wasn't asking about wounds.

'Because Manolito has no more pity than an animal.' He paused, then:

'What exactly happened?'

Magnus told him.

Rhodes understood immediately. 'He's crafty too. The carcass — he'd say the boy was rustling.'

'It was on my land, my cattle!' Magnus said.

'I don't doubt it. Nobody in town'll doubt it either, but if you took it to court in the county seat the Combine'd put up a clever lawyer who'd say different.'

'He won't get that far!'

Rhodes said nothing. There was no point in arguing law with a father standing beside his mutilated son. Then the boy started moaning again.

'You'll need some more whiskey,' he said, 'it eases him a little.' He took the half-empty bottle and got a little more into him. 'That'll hold him for a while.' Too much whiskey could kill too, especially a boy who'd never drunk it before.

Rhodes looked up and saw Alice looking at him from the other side of the room, standing, comforting her mother. Her eyes were red but she wasn't weeping now. He nodded slightly. Better to give her hope, especially as he had no idea as to whether the boy would live or not. Then Doc Gabriel arrived and took over, but not before he had consulted Rhodes like a fellow practitioner, asking exactly what he'd done and why. At last he said:

'You did well, especially giving him whiskey and not laudanum. If you'd given him that he could easily have slipped away.'

'And now he won't?'

'Probably not, but he'll suffer the torments of the damned in the meantime.'

3

It started with Jim Olson approaching him in the barroom and turned into an impromptu council meeting. Olson had been looking for Brand and found both him and his deputy missing. Rhodes told him — and the rest of the council, who'd gradually drifted in — what he knew.

'You'll not see Brand again,' Rhodes concluded. 'He's either dead or departed. I'd guess the first, it's cheaper.'

That didn't seem to trouble them overmuch. Rhodes wasn't surprised. Lawmen rarely inspire vast affection. The spur line did though, some of them seeing it as a very good thing. Rhodes quickly disabused them.

'If the town were to be the railhead, yes, but it isn't. The point is to consolidate all the grazing north of the Buttes into one vast range and drive the smaller ranchers out. This town lives by servicing the smaller ranches.' They saw the logic of that quickly enough.

Rhodes remembered the cheroots in his pocket and lit one, leaning against the bar and listening to them argue, knowing all along just how it would end. They were the city council and they confused that with real power. They passed a motion and then it was carried out, but they'd forgotten how restricted their dominion really was. So, almost unanimously they offered him the post of marshal — the fancier 'chief of police' was forgotten in the panic — and he turned them down.

'You saw what they did to the boy,' Jim Olson said in a disappointed voice.

'Say I were marshal. I arrest Manolito, bring him before you. You'll hang him?'

'No, felonies go to the county seat. I'm only a magistrate.'

'And before a packed jury with a bought judge, what happens to him? He whipped a boy caught rustling. It sounds almost benign. He'd walk and you know it.'

'So he doesn't get that far,' Olson said.

'That's not law but vigilance committee stuff,' Rhodes said. 'It would also be the opening shot of a range war and there too you're outgunned.'

'We can match their guns,' one of the councilmen said.

'In numbers, I don't doubt,' Rhodes said, 'but even if you killed Manolito and all his gang, what then? Gun hands come cheap. They could replace them all in an hour.'

'We have title to our land!' somebody stated.

'True,' Rhodes said, 'and that's your strength. Hang on to what you have. And I'll do the same.' He paused. 'That's why they killed George Wilson. Access to the valley and so to the new railhead was through his — now, my — land. And I don't need a badge to refuse them that, and without it everything else fails.

'Don't try to send out posses on the range. That's acting *ultra vires*. You've no authority outside the city limits and neither does your marshal.'

He didn't add that sending out a posse of shopkeepers and bartenders would be like the mice belling the cat. It was the wrong time and the wrong place for such things to be said. They were all angry men with guns on their hips and whiskey in their bellies and they thought they were invincible.

In the end Jim Olson summed it up for them all:

'It seems to me you're afraid to take on the job of marshal, Rhodes. Very well, we'll find someone who isn't.'

'Then God help him — and you!' Rhodes said and left them to it.

4

Alice met him outside as he was leaving the bar. The spectators were long gone now. It had been a long, weary day and suddenly she was conscious she was wearing her old grey working-dress and not the one she'd picked out for Sunday Meeting — and meeting him.

She knew what he'd told them; gossip like that spread through the small town like wildfire, especially to the doctor's office.

'How is he?' Rhodes said.

'He's better. He's in a lot of pain but he's properly conscious now. Doc Gabriel's hopeful.'

Rhodes nodded. Things happened quickly at that age. You died or you snapped back.

'Come and see him,' she said. 'He'd like to see you.'

'I doubt your pa would. Haven't you

heard, I just don't have the stomach to be marshal?'

'I don't believe that.'

'Heck, I missed seeing you at church,' he said suddenly.

She smiled, the first time that day.

'Not the best way of putting it, I suppose,' Rhodes said, smiling back. 'But I've seen you now.' He paused briefly. 'You're staying in town?'

'Overnight at least. I'll see you tomorrow?'

'I'll try and get back. I've only got Miles at the ranch.'

'And we've only got Derry. Pa will want to get home too.'

'Talk him out of it.'

'But Derry — '

'Will be all right. The Combine may want to buy you out still. The chances are the pressure will be elsewhere if you don't push. Persuade your pa to stay in town.'

'I'll try,' she said.

'I'll be seeing you,' he said and walked quickly away. He'd wanted to say more, do more, but he'd be damned before he would outside a saloon with perhaps half the town watching.

Alice was something special.

PART SIX
LA HORA DE LA SANGRE

1

Adies stood on the rise above La Casa Colorada and looked out on to the range. There was little to see in the dawn light, just pale grass. Not even cattle. They were all to the north now, and that was to the good. He liked it so, not the emptiness of the land — just the emptiness.

Soon enough he would leave this place. It was only a means to an end: getting richer. He'd started life as a gambler and this was all a gamble too, but he rigged the deck very well. He'd kept the town in ignorance, dealt every card from the bottom of the deck.

That was the only way to gamble — to take the luck out of it, otherwise it turned on you. Skill and talent were all very well but you just couldn't beat luck. The sensible gambler soon learned that and took all the luck out of the game. He'd done that, first on river-boats, now here with this empty land.

Take, don't give. That was the sum of the law, the real law, not the footling little law of the ranchers and the townspeople. The suckers. They'd break their backs taming horses and raising cattle and die as naked and poor as they came into the world. It was what they were born for. They were sheep to be fleeced.

But even sheep can get fractious and this new man, this Rhodes, was causing trouble. Brand must have talked to him. Why? What had Brand to gain by talking?

He shrugged. Brand was gone, of no more account now than a broken blade of grass. The news was out and there'd be a little trouble with Gauntsville.

It happened. When the suckers found out they weren't getting an even break, they cut up rough. A sensible gambler took precautions. On the riverboats he'd employed a pair of guards, a couple of ex-plantation straw bosses much exercised in the use of gun, whip and knife. Here, he'd ten times that number, the scourings of the Border towns where you could buy a killing for fifty bucks and a bottle of cheap whiskey.

He'd paid and got the best — Manolito Cahane. Even the stone-killers around him feared Manolito because he truly enjoyed his work. Adies smiled to himself. That, rather than the money was his true hold over his ramrod.

Manolito was no fool. He would have hanged along with his less passionate but hardly less efficient brother, Josefino — 'Joe the Deputy' they called him now! — if it hadn't been for Adies. Yet there was no gratitude in their relationship. Manolito had accepted the bit and tolerated the reins Adies had put on him, and which he loosed a little every so often, because he knew he was safe that way. He found it more than pleasant to kill and maim and he obeyed the boss who allowed him to do it with impunity.

Maybe it was time to loose them

now? Adies thought. But not in town. That would be folly, just too many witnesses. But everywhere outside it, why not? The real law was far away and buyable, and Manolito wasn't one to leave witnesses anyway.

Yes, the time for sleight and duplicity had passed. Now it was time to put a little fear in their hearts. Adies took a parting glance at the green desolation of the range, so empty of everything but himself, and turned back for the Casa Colorada.

Yes, he'd loose his dogs, he decided. His expression didn't change. There was no pleasure in it for him. He had never been one of those gamblers who took enjoyment in watching the punters squirm. That too was folly. You took them down because they were there to be taken, because you wanted what they had.

Everything they had.

2

Rhodes hadn't slept much that night and around two he thought he'd heard the sound of horses on the trail. He didn't go out to see. By the time he'd climbed the rise there'd be nothing to see ... but it made sense. If the Combine had disposed of Brand, it meant they had other sources of information in Gauntsville. And the rider — riders — meant there was news. Maybe just that the secret was out, but maybe something more. Perhaps the kid had taken a turn for the worse? Or maybe something else. His money was on the latter. He slept after that.

In the morning he didn't go into town. It felt like he was breaking his word to Alice but at least he knew she was safe there. He sent Miles into town for supplies — and news, letting him take the rig for the supplies. He gave him cash to pay for them.

'I don't know how my credit stands at the moment.'

'Higher than mine,' Miles said. 'And I'll keep my ears open.'

'By the way, take for your booze out of that.'

Miles looked at him. 'I might buy extra.'

'No you won't,' Rhodes said.

' 'Maybe so.'

'Are you taking that Colt cannon with you?'

'Any objection?'

'I'll buy you a better.'

'I'm used to it. I had one just like it in the war, a Southern copy of course, but none the worse for that. It worked.'

★   ★   ★

When Miles had left Rhodes settled himself down on the near side of the rise with a canteen of water and a Sharps rifle. The horse-breaking could wait a day. The rifle could shoot twenty times as far as a handgun and far beyond the range of even a Winchester carbine: from there he could control the trail.

He smoked cheroot after cheroot and waited, three cartridges lying on the ground beside the rifle ready for use. He didn't expect to need them. He'd only brought the rifle out of old habit. When you were on watch, you made sure you were ready for all eventualities. And, mostly, nothing at all happened.

He wasn't even sure why he was here. Nothing would happen in town — he wouldn't have sent Miles otherwise — and there was no real reason to expect Manolito and his bunch to come riding up to the ranch, guns blazing. He'd just had a gut feeling that something was out of kilter. Whatever, it would be interesting to see if anyone did ride off the range into town.

No one did. There was no movement either way until he saw Miles coming back with the loaded rig.

Miles stopped on the crest.

'That's one hell of a gun for shooting prairie dogs,' he said.

Rhodes glanced in the back of the rig, saw the sacks and boxes and the six bottles of whisky. That wasn't excessive for a drinker for a month. 'Any problems?'

'No. Once I started to pay cash, they wanted to offer credit.'

'How's the boy?'

'Better.'

'So what else?'

'They've got a new marshal. Brand's as forgotten as if he'd just passed through for a day thirty years ago.'

Who?'

'Magnus Sims.'

'Damn!' Rhodes said.

'There's no talk of posses,' Miles said. 'All they've done is give him a badge.'

'So long as he stays in town . . . '

'Ah,' Miles said.

'Go on. Questioning you is like pulling teeth.'

'Well,' Miles said, 'he's not. He's going home today.'

'All of them?'

'The boy's staying, so is the mother.'

'When?'

'They were putting supplies on their wagon when I left.'

Rhodes bent and scooped up loose ammunition, slipped it in his pocket, took up the gun and climbed aboard the rig.

'I'll ride with you to the barn. I need to saddle up a horse.'

'Can I be of service?' Miles asked, starting the rig moving.

'Not yet. Just get the supplies away and enter 'em in the accounts.'

'And what will you be doing?'

'Watching. And maybe praying . . . '

3

They came up the trail early in the afternoon, Magnus driving and Alice beside him looking distinctly unhappy. Rhodes was tempted to mount up and join them but he restrained himself and kept out of sight. Magnus Sims would as likely as not send him packing and that would only complicate things. Besides, he'd be far more use shadowing them from a distance. The odds were already far too high in the Combine's favour. He needed to do all he could to balance them.

He let them pass, using the time to roll a cigarette. There was no need for haste. Magnus, true rancher that he was, had taken the opportunity to get his supplies in. The wagon was well laden and only crawling along. He might be wearing a star but that was all: he didn't think like a peace officer. It was all too obvious that he imagined the badge itself gave power, not realizing that all it gave was a measure of impunity afterwards. They mostly didn't hang peace officers.

Rhodes found himself thinking about his advice to the town . . . do nothing, wait. Good advice or just his own stubborn streak breaking through? The question was unanswerable. He crushed out his cigarette underfoot and walked back to his tethered horse a little lower down the rise. It was time to start trailing the wandering marshal.

*　*　*

In one thing Marshal Sims showed sense. He didn't venture far out on to the range but kept as close to the Peak side as he could, which meant Rhodes had to keep closer, making it much harder for him. Part of the time he had to dismount and walk his horse through scrubland, keeping an eye out for potholes while still taking care to keep well out of sight of the wagon. There was little chance of him losing it. It's progress was too fixed and too slow for that.

After an hour he fancied nothing was going to happen. Manolito might well still be at the Casa Colorada or even cowboying the Combine's substantial herd. And then, in the distance, he heard voices raised. The temptation was to mount up and ride but again he resisted it. Another twenty yards and they would be in sight. He quickened his pace and walked on, still watchful for potholes that might lame his horse and strand him.

And then he saw them, the wagon stopped on the off-trail, the three riders close around it, and Magnus leaning forward and shouting.

As he watched, Magnus reached for the shotgun he carried on the wagon but Manolito was too close. The *pistola* flashed out of its belly holster, not to shoot but to club the old rancher. Up and down, flashing in the afternoon sunlight.

Magnus slumped forward in his seat. So much for the value of a marshal's badge.

The attention then turned to Alice. She raised the buggy whip but it was torn from her hands and then one of them lifted her bodily from the wagon and deposited her on the grass. Rhodes could hear laughter. He was in no doubt as to what they intended next. The tightness in his stomach wasn't fear but anger, the coldest killing rage he had ever felt in his life.

Rhodes took his Sharps rifle from its sheath and raised the sights, estimating the distance automatically. The air was still, so there was no windage to account for. He raised the weapon to his shoulder and aimed — at Manolito who was bending over the supine form of Alice, holding her by the arm.

It had to be a careful shot, a head shot, not the more certain torso shot that he would have preferred. He let out his breath, keeping the rifle rock-steady, and gently, very gently squeezed the trigger.

Manolito's black sombrero jumped into the air as he was plucked off Alice and flung backwards by the heavy bullet.

Carefully, Rhodes reloaded. The other two were confused, not knowing where the shot had come from. He aimed, fired again. This time the luxury of a head shot wasn't required and the heavy bullet hit the second gunhand like a sledgehammer, flinging him into the air . . . and dropping then like a load of old clothes.

The third gunhand mounted up and used his spurs. Let him go? The idea died quickly as Rhodes thought of what he — what they had all — intended for Alice. He had never shot a fleeing man before but this was different. And there was no hurry. A rifle bullet couldn't be evaded even on a galloping horse. He loaded, rechecked the distance, adjusted the sights and fired.

And missed. He'd underestimated the distance. He reloaded again, adjusted the sights again and fired. The man's head virtually exploded. But he hadn't been aiming for the head. The rifle was firing high, he noted.

He let out his breath, and a little of the anger, and walked his horse towards the wagon. Let Alice have a minute to compose herself, he thought. It was only decent.

When he got there she had forgotten about herself and was tending to her father.

'How is he?'

'He's alive!'

He was, Rhodes thought, and likely to remain so. He'd seen worse pistol-whippings. Manolito's mind hadn't been on his work.

'Oh, Tom!' she said and suddenly she was in his arms.

'Hush,' he said softly, holding her. Her father groaned, another good sign, and she half-turned. Then, 'Oh God, Tom — !'

Rhodes broke free and turned to see Manolito rising as if from the dead, his blond hair slick and dark now, his face a mask of blood but staring out from it the dark eyes were very, very clear. The shot had only creased his head. Just an inch lower and it would have taken off the top of his skull. Damn the rifle! All the same he wished it were in his hands at this moment and not back in the sheath.

Rhodes reached out instantly, caught Alice by the shoulder, threw her to the ground to his left, then stepped in front of her as he drew.

Manolito was also drawing the *pistola* from its belly holster and he was incredibly fast — it was a trick holster, split and spring-held so you could pull the whole barrel out through the holster in one motion.

Rhodes was unsurprised. It was the kind of cheap gunsel trick a would-be rapist-murderer like Manolito Cahane would try, and like all tricks it had its drawbacks. It worked better when your opponent was unsuspecting and didn't move. By moving to the left to protect Alice, by the time Manolito had his gun out it was aimed to Rhodes' right by the very motion of drawing it.

It wasn't much of an edge but Rhodes' own gun was in his hand and aimed straight at Manolito's chest. He didn't hesitate.

Crack! The heavy bullet caught Manolito full on and Rhodes walked inexorably forward, cocking and firing, cocking and firing. The figure with its blood-masked face twisted and turned under the deluge of hammer-blows like the puppet of a drunken puppeteer, ever trying to bring the *pistola* on target until it finally fell from his nerveless fingers as Manolito himself collapsed. Rhodes was above him then, still cocking and firing, full of a hate he had never felt before — for a man he had killed six times over.

Rhodes wrenched himself back, holstered his gun and turned to her, now on her feet again but white as a ghost.

'That bastard will never threaten you again,' he said. Then: 'Let's get your father back to the ranch. Tie my horse to the wagon.'

Out of curiosity he went and picked up Manolito's sombrero and saw the bullet had passed through the felt but had hardly damaged it. He kept it and on impulse stripped the holster from the corpse and retrieved the gun before tying Manolito's horse to the wagon too. It was well used to gunfire. It had not moved at all during the fight.

He helped Alice up to sit beside her father and then climbed aboard himself, making a long U-turn back towards his own ranch leaving the bodies as they were, for the coyotes.

4

Magnus Sims had a hard head and was conscious again by the time they bumped over the rise and saw the horse ranch before them. He was even bleating about going home. Rhodes ignored him. He could cure him of that folly easily enough, by getting him on his own and pointing out that his own judgement had almost got himself killed and his daughter raped, and then left with her throat cut out on the prairie. Even Magnus's hard head wouldn't be hard enough to withstand that argument. But it could wait. Maybe it wouldn't even be needed.

When Miles arrived to help, Rhodes outlined the situation in a very few words. For a moment Miles's jaw set in a way that resolved any last doubt he'd had of him.

As it turned out there was no need to

argue with Magnus, as he suddenly turned very tired and sleepy. Alice was worried — unduly, Rhodes thought, but he made no major effort to stop her playing nurse. Better she worry about her father than herself.

'Hungry?' Miles asked.

'No,' Rhodes said, 'but thanks anyway. I think I'll get some air.' The house was suddenly too confining. It had too many memories — of a boyhood that he had done his best to forget, not for any horrors but for its coldness and aridity. 'I'll see to the stock,' he said. 'You hang about and keep an eye on our guests.'

'Okay, they'll be fine.'

So were the horses. After a while Rhodes retreated to the coral fence, leaning on it as he rolled a cigarette. He had problems to think through.

He'd had no choice in his actions but he knew the Combine would consider what he'd done as a declaration of war. There was just no getting around that, nor the fact that they could field twenty guns in the hands of men who knew how to use them, even double their number in short order. What was the going rate for a killing — a hundred dollars? With railroad money behind them they could put fifty men in the field. Of course, the town could telegraph the federal marshal and the county sheriff, but who was to say a little railroad money hadn't touched their palms too, not to join in on either side but simply to be very, very slow in reacting? If the complainants were dead there was, *ipso facto*, no complaint.

Maybe he was misjudging them both but, for all he had been an honest lawman himself, he had no illusions. The job didn't pay well, had no pension to speak of, and inaction was always pretty easy to buy.

So take the town marshal's job? Magnus would yield it up easily now, he knew. But what good would that do? The badge hadn't gained him anything, quite the reverse. No, that wasn't the road to go down. If they just hoped for the best, waited for the Combine to make its play, they were lost. Action was called for, and fast.

Form a posse? It could be done — Miles, Derry Sims, maybe half a dozen small ranchers and two or three men from town. But that was on the topside and they'd be still outnumbered two to one by men better at the job of fighting and killing than themselves, quite possibly with the law on *their* side. Rhodes didn't confuse right and law for one instant.

He hadn't lit the cigarette and the tobacco was seeping out at one end. He folded it over and found his lucifers, then changed his mind and crumpled the depleted cigarette up into a ball and tossed it aside.

There was one possible course of action and he'd known it all along. So had Miles, and Alice too — at least she would if she let herself think about it. Manolito hadn't simply been acting on his own account. He'd been given orders. The man that gave them was no whit less responsible than his late ramrod and had to be dealt with no less severely.

Rhodes felt no compunction whatever. He hadn't started this but he fully intended to survive it, and what had so nearly happened to Alice was something he'd never forget or forgive.

He admitted to himself that it was about even more than survival. In a sense he hardly knew her and yet it was truly much more than that; it was as if she'd been waiting here for his return, the one absolutely decent thing in this valley, and they'd tried to despoil and destroy her. That was much more than legality or even survival. He'd been sick when he'd first killed in the war and he'd gone out of his way to avoid putting notches on his gun as a deputy, but this was different.

He stopped himself, suddenly realising the depth of his feelings for her, a girl he'd only met a few times. It just didn't seem reasonable. He smiled, briefly. It wasn't reasonable at all. But it was real.

He rolled himself another cigarette and lit it this time, leaning on the fence and looking over his little kingdom, knowing she was in the house safe and sound.

He knew exactly what he had to do.

5

Her father was sleeping normally again. For all he'd come to in the wagon, he'd all but collapsed in the house. A slight concussion, Rhodes had said. She'd believed him in a way but had worried too. Now, just seeing her father lying there in his clothes, *sans* boots, on Miles's bed in the barely furnished back bedroom, somehow set her mind at rest.

She'd wanted to let Derry know, but Rhodes had disagreed and she could see his point. Derry would only abandon the ranch *in extremis*, which thankfully this wasn't, and there was no risk that he'd come looking because he wasn't expecting them back early anyway. And Derry was a patient man, almost to excess. All the same, it didn't seem right just to ignore him.

Suddenly her father started snoring.

For a second she almost froze, thinking he was having breathing difficulties, but it was just common or garden snoring. She sighed. He'd sleep himself well just as Tom Rhodes had said.

And Sean would be fine too. The doctor hadn't said so straight out but she'd read him well enough. Sean would make it because Tom Rhodes had saved his life.

Just as he had saved hers, and more. She tried not to think about that — it had been so swift, so horrible, she hadn't really had time to react to it when it was happening. But she had time now. She took a breath and considered going into hysterics. Except she didn't know how. She also knew it would do no good. Nothing had happened, thanks to Tom.

She found herself thinking of Manolito flung from her, the distant killing of the other two: death reaching out from nowhere and touching them . . . and then the killing, the second killing, of Manolito himself.

Tom had been like an avenging angel, full of cold fury. It had shocked her at the time and did again now. She realized she didn't know him at all, and yet she knew exactly why he had been so angry. Not for her father, he'd helped him just as he'd helped Sean, but he'd kill for neither of them. He'd killed for her.

That frightened her, and thrilled her too. In the dime novels of romance she'd read at Normal School — not as part of the curriculum — it would have been a distinct plus in a man. But in real life?

Her father or either of her brothers would have done the same — or tried to. Tom was simply better at it. And Manolito had deserved everything he'd got and more, not only for her but for Sean. Much more for Sean, for she'd had only a second's fright. Sean had been almost beaten to death. No, Tom had been right and she was crazy for having thought otherwise.

She hadn't just set her cap for Tom, it

was more than that. She'd known from the first. And so had he. His fury hadn't been born out of cruelty, quite the reverse. And here she was being stupid and girlish and, worst of all, thinking too much. There were things you could make better by thinking about them, but this wasn't one of those. Feeling was enough. Caring was enough.

Tom had followed her because he was afraid for her, and rightly so as it had turned out. He had been one against three and he'd used his old skills as a soldier and sheriff and killed, and she was glad they were dead. It was horrible and disloyal to castigate him for the killing, even in the privacy of her own mind.

How must he be feeling? She tried to imagine but she was too tired and confused and even as her father snored contentedly in the small bed he dwarfed, she found herself weeping silently.

She wiped her eyes the better to keep her vigil but soon enough she was sleeping too, silently, on the chair by the bed.

6

Alice awoke in the pre-dawn light, stiff from the chair, but her first thought was for her father. He was sleeping normally. He looked bruised but otherwise well. Then she heard movement in the next room. There was no mirror so she tidied her hair as best she could and ventured forth.

The room smelt of coffee but not of cooking. Both Tom and Miles were dressed, the former drinking out of a tin mug, spilling ash from his cigarette on the hard earth floor. It had obviously been a long time since a woman had lived in this house.

'Morning,' Tom said. Miles echoed the greeting but paid her no attention otherwise. He said to Rhodes:

'Let me go with you.'

Rhodes shook his head. 'No, you stay, it'll be easier for me on my own.'

He said it casually but somehow she knew that it was an order none the less, the end of the matter.

'How's Magnus?' Tom Rhodes asked, looking at her.

'He's fine,' she said, then: 'Where are you going?'

'Maybe to commit a crime,' Rhodes said. 'Or maybe to tend my herd of horses.'

'You know I'd lie for you.'

He looked straight at her. She held his gaze, knowing where he was intending to go. It frightened her but she tried not to let it show.

'You'd make a very poor liar,' he said smiling.

She shook her head mutely.

'We haven't won a great victory out there,' he said suddenly. 'Manolitos are replaceable, and even come cheap. We — I — have to go to the fountainhead.'

'La Casa Colorada,' she said softly.

Rhodes shrugged. 'Your words, not mine.'

'They'll kill you!'

'I have no intention of dying.' He paused, then: 'Can you sew?'

'Of course.'

He went over to a corner table and brought back the sombrero and the holstered *pistola*. He gave her the hat. She took hold of it very gingerly.

'Patch up those holes, please,' he said. 'You'll find needle and thread on the mantelpiece. Nothing elaborate, just so it's not too obvious.'

She found the needle and thread and was about to ask why but he was no longer looking at her, fiddling instead with the holster. She tried to thread the needle and failed. It surprised her. She was usually very good at that.

★   ★   ★

Rhodes had hoped to have avoided Alice before leaving. He didn't know why. Not because he was ashamed of what he intended, though there was nothing exactly glorious about it.

He concentrated on the *pistola*

153

holster he'd just strapped on. The mechanism was quite stiff and the pressure needed to release it flung the *pistola* badly to the right. It was altogether a poor system though the gun itself was effective enough. The cartridges had turned out to be just sixteen-gauge but solid shot, with cruciform cuts in them. Very nasty. He was glad his acquaintanceship with Manolito Cahane had been short.

'You're going to kill Adies,' Alice said suddenly.

Rhodes glanced up at her and saw her looking at him with big, concerned eyes.

'You object?'

Her jaw hardened. 'I only wish I could help. Sean and Pa and what . . . ' She broke off, remembering.

Rhodes noticed she still hadn't threaded the needle. He took both needle and thread from her.

'It'll do fine as it is. It'll only work at a distance anyway.' He paused, then: 'You still don't strike me as a good liar.'

She looked at him puzzled.

'I think I'd better marry you. A wife can't testify against her husband.'

And suddenly she was weeping again. Bad timing, Rhodes thought. Then: what the hell! He reached out to her and pulled her to him and felt her hands gripping him with all the strength she had.

Maybe his timing wasn't so far off after all.

PART SEVEN
LA CASA COLORADA

1

Rhodes left with the dawn, riding Manolito's great black horse. He rode hard at first though the horse, a mountain of strength, scarcely seemed to notice. The sombrero was a nuisance and the belly-rigged *pistola* distinctly uncomfortable but as he and Manolito were of a size he felt fairly confident that at a distance he would be taken for him. People tended to see what they expected to see. And Rhodes guessed that few sought out Manolito unasked.

Perhaps it was riding into the dawn, or maybe it was just plain fear that brought it back, but he found himself recollecting a similar ride in the Carolinas in the closing year of the war. They'd been brigaded with another regiment of Volunteer Cavalry and he'd been leading the troop of which he was acting-captain, except it was a troop more in name than in numbers. He had just twenty-six men behind him and the whole brigade probably didn't have more than 500 riders, if that.

There had been reports of Confederate cavalry regiments in the vicinity and the divisional general had ordered a reconnaissance in force. The objective was seven miles off, an hour's canter in better times but their horses were no less tired than the men and they took most of it at the walk, over lush green fields with here and there a copse where infantry might be hiding. Fortunately his regiment had been in the lead in the last advance and the order had been switched, otherwise the chances were his troop would have been on point, detailed to check the copses out.

Every time they stopped the tension was palpable; the troopers were waiting for the point to be shattered by a sudden discharge of rifles and then the order given to take the *franc-tireurs* at the charge.

But the copses had held no holdouts

or snipers and the order to advance was given again, snapping through the brigade like a faulty drum roll.

He hadn't looked back once that morning, telling himself his men would be there come what may, but really afraid to turn in case they saw the fear in his face. It was mounting with the sun. And with the fear was a growing certainty that this would be his last battle, that the bullet with his name on it was already cast and loaded in a Reb rifle. He'd never had the feeling so strongly before, not even when they'd charged the flank at Leyden Hill, and he found himself regretting that he'd let them promote him. It was a fine thing to wear a pair of bars and ride ahead but given the choice that morning he'd have much preferred to be in the rearmost rank, ready to run off if need be.

He knew the rank would mean very little after the war. The army would shrink a hundredfold, back to its previous size and the West Pointers would take over at troop level. He'd be counting himself lucky just to get his back-pay. Not that he wanted to stay in. He wished he were out now and so, he reckoned, did every single one of his troop. If the Rebs were saving their fusillades now, they'd be worse later, much worse.

In the end the seven miles were traversed and their objective was in sight. But there was no charge. There was only one horse there, a poor, spavined creature tied up to a tent peg. It was a Confederate field hospital abandoned to the enemy for lack of transport and as they drew near they could smell the sickly sweetness of gangrene and filth in the air. Yet despite that he'd felt a sense of elation he'd never felt before. The fear had fallen away instantly and he'd suddenly known that he would survive. Even when he'd gone inside the tents to supervise the distribution of water — the senior colonel had ordered every other canteen to be donated — and seen sights out of Dante's *Inferno* it hadn't affected his mood. He was alive and he would come through.

He had. The bullet might have been cast but it was never fired. He had spent the rest of the war, what little of it there was, matching men and remounts and had never heard another shot fired in anger.

★ ★ ★

The bunch grass was nothing like the sheer green lushness of the Carolinas and he was riding alone, not leading one troop among many. The memory slipped away and his fear with it. Maybe that bullet had been exported out West. Maybe not. It would do no good to think about it. He'd done all he could, ridden on another man's horse, worn his hat and carried his gun and, as it had turned out so far, needlessly. He'd seen no one on the prairie and no one had seen him. Maybe it would be different now with the Casa Colorada in plain sight.

2

Until he'd first seen it as a boy Rhodes had supposed the Casa Colorada to have once been a Spanish mission. But it was just a ranch, so named because its first owner, Diego Domingo, long dead now, had been of Spanish stock and had painted his ranch house red.

Red was a good colour to withstand wind and weather. In thirty years nobody had ever repainted it so in parts the great house was near black and in others a rather sickly pink. But no one had ever cared to retitle it the 'Casa Rosa' — 'colorada' it had remained.

Rhodes slowed his horse's pace. His plan was brutally simple: kill the snake by cutting off its head. In legal terms, to murder Adies. But the law was no longer applicable. Adies himself had declared war on him and his when he sent Manolito to kill his uncle and rape

164

Alice. Different rules applied now. Call it vengeance or wild justice but it really amounted to simple survival. Rhodes found he had no qualms whatsoever.

The Casa Colorada ranch was a complex of buildings, the old house on the low rise and the three barns, bunkhouse and corral below. The trail up to the house was clearly visible from below so Rhodes kept his head forward so that no one below could see his face. The couple of people about paid him no attention. They'd seen Manolito ride in many times before.

He reached the house and dismounted, tying up his horse to the hitching rail. Then he walked straight in through the front door. A Mexican woman scurried up to greet him. He kept his head down.

'Señor Manolito, *el* Señor Adies *está* — '

'Get lost!' Rhodes snarled, not caring to risk his Spanish and hoping the vicious tone would make up for any other deficiency of expression. He'd never heard Manolito speak.

It seemed to work. The woman scurried off and Rhodes, relying on dregs of memory, started for the salon where he judged Adies would be. He came quickly to the polished double-doors, opened them and stepped inside.

No Adies, only lawyer Sandfort, by the fireplace, his hands full of papers he was about to burn on an otherwise unneeded fire. More papers lay scattered all over the great table in the room's centre.

'Mano — ' Sandfort began, and stopped. Rhodes didn't: he ran the three paces up to the lawyer and knocked him away from the fire. What the Combine wanted burnt, he just wanted.

Sandfort had landed heavily and the papers had fallen from his flaccid hands. Rhodes scooped them up. Then he glanced behind him — the doors were ajar and there was no one there — before he looked Sandfort over. He was out to the world. Had he recognised him? Very probably, which was a nuisance to say the least.

He looked at the papers. They were of two sorts: correspondence on letter-headed sheets and estimates on plain sheets. He examined the letter-headed sheets first. Most were from the railroad company, a correspondence about the spur line. From what he skimmed it wouldn't make pleasant reading for the Gauntsville Council. The railhead wasn't to be in the valley but outside on land already bought cheaply. The bridge would be for people and cattle only. There was more financial stuff he'd have to ponder over to make any sense of it.

The sheets without letter-heads were pretty obviously based on cattle tallies, but something happened between the left-and right-hand sides of the paper. The figures doubled. So the Combine was cheating the railroad people too, overestimating to get the line built. Once it was built the railroad company would have little choice but to keep it running to make something out of their investment. No wonder Adies wanted these disposed of.

In fact, now he had them, he needn't perhaps kill Adies at all. Maybe, seeing these, the railroad company would happily do the job for him, financially at least. Or maybe even in the flesh.

'Drop the papers, Rhodes!'

Rhodes had turned away from the lawyer to catch the light on the papers.

'I've a gun on you.'

Quite possible. He didn't wear a six-gun rig but he could well have a derringer or a pocket pistol of some sort. Rhodes tossed the papers on the table using the opportunity to cock the *pistola* and grasp it. Sandfort couldn't have moved, other than to raise himself partly up or Rhodes would have heard him.

'Now what?' Rhodes asked.

'Now we wait,' Sandfort said. 'Turn around.'

Rhodes turned, fired as the *pistola* bore on Sandfort, angling it down. Fired in its holster the noise was deafening and the belly rig jarred painfully against him.

The cruciform bullet took Sandfort in the chest, punching a hole through it. He flung his arms in the air and the derringer sailed over Rhodes to land by the door. Then Rhodes noticed his own shirt was on fire. He beat it out with his hands. The belly rig might have saved his life but it still had its disadvantages.

He glanced at Sandfort's corpse without regret. Lawyers shouldn't play with guns — or murder. But he did regret the noise. The house was on the alert now. There was no chance of catching Adies unprepared. Better for him to cut his losses, take the papers and ride.

He gathered them up from the table, taking everything that was there, folding them up and stuffing them down his now less than pristine shirt front. As he walked to the door he stooped to pick up the derringer, noting that it hadn't even been cocked. Sandfort had been doubly foolish but that was his look-out. The derringer fired a heavy bullet quite as nasty as the *pistola*'s at short range. Sandfort had been prepared to use it, he'd been just no good at it.

For a moment Rhodes considered tossing it by the body, leaving evidence that it wasn't murder. He smiled briefly at himself. That was peace officer thinking. If they caught him they'd shoot him anyway, and there was just no way they'd respect the evidence. Also, he still hadn't reloaded the *pistola* or even checked that it still worked after being so unceremoniously used. The derringer was the only working weapon he had, his own six-gun rig safe and for now useless in his saddle-bags.

He went out the way he'd come. No one got in the way or even in his sight. Rhodes guessed there was no one but servants in the house, the Mexicans brought by Diego Domingo all those years ago and their descendants, and they weren't about to get mixed up in *Anglo* shooting-matches.

Adies was probably down by the barns or the bunkhouse. As soon as they felt it was safe the staff would be running down there reporting. The shooting might even have been heard down there already. He was better on his way.

The black horse was waiting where he'd left it, quite unfazed by the noise. Typical of Manolito's horse, he thought, mounting up and heading down the rise for the open range and safety.

3

Adies tried to make sense of Maria's Spanish and failed. It was too fast and confused. He looked to Joe the Deputy.

'She says it was Manolito.'

Adies shook his head. That made no sense. 'She saw his face? How did he sound?'

More lightning fast Spanish, then:

'No, and he sounded odd. He even spoke English to her.' Joe the Deputy paused, then said, 'But it was his horse and he was wearing the *pistola* and a sombrero.'

'But she didn't see his face?'

'No.'

'Not Manolito,' Adies decided.

'No, he is dead,' the big man said without emotion. Adies glanced at him. Josefino Cahane Murieta was talking about his brother. Adies wondered just what he felt. The brothers had never shown affection for anyone. Adies pushed the matter aside. Of infinitely more importance were the papers. By the look of the fireplace few if any had been burnt. Whoever had them could put at least a financial noose around his neck. He considered. Probably Rhodes. Brand had been excessively nervous of him, one of the reasons for disposing of him. But it didn't matter who. All that mattered was getting the papers back.

'How many men have we here now?' Adies had twenty-three riders all told but there were also 4,000 beeves out on the range. It seemed good economy to use the gunhands as cowboys too . . . until they were needed for their true function.

'Three.'

'Leave two here — they might be trying to draw us off — and meet me at the base of the rise in two minutes.'

'I can kill him myself,' Joe the Deputy said, not quite without inflection.

'I don't doubt it,' Adies said. He

didn't, but he added: 'All our necks are on the line so it's better to be safe than sorry.' Manolito had been the flashier of the two brothers but there was a terrible, unemotional implacability about Joe the Deputy. Adies thought it wise to add: 'When we get him, he's yours.'

'*Sí*, patron.' The big Mexican nodded and left.

Adies took one last look at Lawyer Sandfort before going to collect his guns. The lawyer had been unlucky but he'd been a man born to be hanged if there ever was one. At least he'd avoided that fate.

4

They were gaining on him — three of them, one of them unmistakably Joe the Deputy. If only he had his Sharps rifle . . . but he'd decided not to risk it. Manolito hadn't carried a rifle. As it turned out, that wouldn't have mattered . . . but it could have. No plan worked out as intended: he remembered that from the war. But he hadn't lost yet.

He eased back on the reins, let the big animal slow to a walk. He couldn't compete with their fresh horses. With Adies dead it wouldn't have mattered: gunhands had no loyalty to a dead paymaster.

He took out the *pistola* and found it still good. He cut away the straps of the holster rig with his knife, slipping the spare cartridges into his pocket and, after reloading, the *pistola* into his belt.

He reached back for the six-gun rig in his saddle-bags, which he fastened on. Three guns, including the derringer in his pocket, for three opponents. It had a nice symmetry to it, if nothing else.

He needed somewhere to make a stand. A cluster of rocks or a clump of trees would be best but he didn't need to glance round to know that all there was to be found was lightly grassed flat land, with just the occasional stunted bush that wouldn't have provided good cover for a prairie dog. And then he remembered — McAleer's Dip.

You couldn't see it until you were almost upon it for a dip was all it was — eight feet deep in the centre and the sides tapering up for over a hundred yards. And it was only half a mile away to the south.

He glanced back. The three of them had reined in too — keeping their horses fresh though they were still gaining on him. But not too quickly: there was still a chance of surprising them. He set the horse to a canter and then quickly to a gallop, veering south. Suddenly the odds were looking a lot more even.

'Come on,' he cajoled the great black brute, 'one more effort and you can rest and graze. Don't let me down.'

It didn't. It had even opened up the gap to 400 yards. They must have been surprised to see him one moment and not the next, Rhodes thought as he lay on the edge of the dip, the *pistola* in his hand, watching.

They'd stopped 300 yards off and were talking among themselves. If the *pistola* had half the range of a Sharps rifle he could have taken one of them for certain, two maybe, but fifty yards with an aimed shot was about the best he could expect. At least, they didn't know he didn't have a long arm.

Their best plan was to come at him from three sides — they must suspect he'd found a dip in the land — and yet they seemed reluctant to do so. He knew why. It was basic military strategy not to divide your forces in the presence of the enemy. Wrong for once but let them not believe it!

His prayer was answered. They came in a rush, three together, shooting to put him off his aim. It didn't. They couldn't see him and their shots were wild. He didn't return fire, just waited. When they were a hundred yards off he fired his first shot, aiming high and hoping for the best.

It missed but he reloaded quickly and fired again, high still. One of the riders seemed to jump backwards off his horse as if hit by an invisible hand. Rhodes didn't waste time rejoicing, just reloaded. The barrel of the *pistola* was getting hot.

The remaining pair were riding almost straight at him but he guessed they hadn't seen him yet. He fired again.

A horse fell, pitching its rider forward — Joe the Deputy. With luck he'd have broken his neck. Rhodes dropped the *pistola*, drew his six-gun and turned to face the rider who was almost upon him — a medium-sized man in a suit, a man with red hair, grey at the temples, and a six-gun in his hand firing straight at him. Adies.

Rhodes rose up and fired, fanning the gun at the oncoming rider, unfazed by the incoming fire. Being fired at from horseback it would be pure bad luck if he were hit.

He wasn't. Adies was. A .44 bullet caught him in the face and Rhodes saw blood and brains spurt out from the back of his skull. He must have jerked involuntarily on the reins for the horse shied up and the body fell lifeless to the grass. Rhodes felt a sudden exhilaration. He'd taken on impossible odds and won.

The exhilaration didn't last.

'You killed Manolito.'

Rhodes turned and saw Joe the Deputy fifteen feet away. He pointed his six-gun and pulled the trigger.

Click! An empty chamber. They were all empty.

'I counted,' Joe the Deputy said,

without inflection, keeping his gun levelled as he walked closer to him.

Rhodes thought of the derringer in his pocket but his chances of getting to it were zero. He could only wait.

'He was attempting to rape a woman,' Rhodes said. 'He didn't manage that either. I killed him before he could fire a shot.' Rhodes had nothing to lose by angering Joe the Deputy and perhaps something to gain.

Joe the Deputy tossed the gun aside, drew a knife. Not a great Bowie knife but a Spanish-style stiletto, its slim blade dwarfed by the massive hand that held it.

Rhodes didn't even attempt to go for the derringer. His opponent was only yards off. Instead he reversed the six-gun, held it like a club.

'You die screaming,' Joe the Deputy said in the same flat tones.

Rhodes backed off, keeping his arms spread to ward off blows. If he could get one blow of his own in, retreat and get out the derringer, the heavy bullet would stop even such a hulk as the one before him.

Joe the Deputy darted forward, extraordinarily quick for a big man, and the knife touched Rhodes' arm, slicing the material of his shirt but no more than scoring his skin.

Rhodes backed away further but his huge opponent followed, the knife darting out with consummate skill, lunges still, not the upward slashing cuts that could disembowel a man.

Rhodes swung his improvised club, caught him on the hand once but it made no difference. The big Mexican seemed impervious to pain. The knife stayed in his hand, darted out again and would have cut into Rhodes' chest if it hadn't been for the papers stuffed there. But Rhodes knew their utility as armour was insufficient. He backed off further.

'*Cobarde!*'

The descent into Spanish suggested his opponent was getting very angry. It made little difference. Rhodes knew he was faced with a supreme knife-fighter — and he himself had no knife. It wasn't cowardly to retreat, hoping for a bit of luck. It would have been insane to do otherwise.

He got his luck — bad luck. He stumbled as his foot caught in a pothole, fell back. Joe the Deputy was above him in an instant, the knife held low for a gutting stroke.

Rhodes flung the useless pistol at Joe the Deputy's face, scrabbling desperately for the derringer and knowing he wouldn't make it.

Joe the Deputy brushed the projectile aside with a motion of his arm, then the knife flashed down.

Crack!

Rhodes heard the shot and instantly saw the spreading blood on Joe the Deputy's chest. A heavy bullet had made that wound, a rifle bullet. It would have knocked another man down. It merely gave Joe the Deputy pause.

'For Manolito!' he screamed and

would have driven the knife down into Rhodes' stomach but the pause had been long enough for Rhodes to get the derringer out.

He shot him in the face, emptying the head like a melon struck by a sledgehammer. Then he rolled quickly away as the mighty body fell, the knife still in the dead hand, uselessly stabbing the green earth.

★ ★ ★

Rhodes watched as Miles came towards him, leading his horse, the Sharps rifle over his shoulder, soldier-fashion.

'Alice is fine,' Miles said. 'She insisted I came out to see if I could be of any help. Magnus is up and about too, and neither is far from a shotgun.'

Rhodes couldn't think what answer to make for a moment, then:

'George Wilson would've been proud of you.'

EPILOGUE

It was an ordinary boardroom but it was the best in Sweetwater. There were three men around a polished mahogany table — Smith, a plain-looking man to head a railroad but a man with quiet authority; his deputy, Reese, all side whiskers and silk cravat; and Rhodes, in a store-bought suit that looked well on him.

'Interesting reading,' Smith said, looking at the papers Rhodes had brought, 'if true. How did you come by them, incidentally?'

'They were given to me,' Rhodes lied.

'That's not the way I hear it,' Reese put in. 'There could be charges of murder and — '

'Let's not worry about that yet,' Smith interrupted his deputy. 'Our concern is business, purely business.'

'Of course, and these — ' Rhodes

gestured — 'show that an attempt has been made to defraud you.'

'If true, yes.'

Rhodes leaned back, took out a cheap cigar and lit it. Reese made a face but said nothing. Eventually Rhodes said:

'As I read it, Adies promised you eight thousand head the first year and more thereafter for your backing of the Combine. He could have managed four thousand at best, and that only by cutting well into his breeding stock. But that wouldn't have mattered to him. He fully intended to sell the land he'd bought once its price had gone up thanks to the coming of the railroad. Then he would have left pronto, leaving you with egg on your face. Agreed?'

'I wouldn't put it quite so colourfully . . . but essentially, yes.'

'So this Manolito who went mad and killed Adies and the rest really did you gentlemen a favour.'

Reese harrumphed.

'There's still a shortfall,' Smith said.

'It could be we've bought land to no purpose.'

'No, build your spur line. The range there can support ten thousand a year easily. The Combine was using force to hog the range north of the Buttes, and then not really exploiting it properly. Let the smaller ranches in on it. What does it matter to you whose cattle you transport? You're a railroad company.'

'And forget several killings?' Reese put in.

Rhodes looked at him. 'I don't doubt you can get me charged but I doubt even a railroad company in a railroad town could get me convicted.'

Reese gestured proprietarily at the papers. 'These could very easily be suppressed.'

'Forget the legalities,' Rhodes said, 'you can have them now. I've no further use for them.'

Smith looked up. 'You're taking a big risk, Mr Rhodes. Why shouldn't we blame it all on you — *railroad* you, if you'll forgive the everyday expression?'

'Because that would still leave you with a shortfall. Okay, maybe you could put together a bought judge and a jury that would convict George Washington, posthumously, of treason, but you couldn't stop people talking — and hearing. Stockholders, for instance. Adies took you for fools.' Rhodes paused to let the point sink in. Then: 'But I've no wish to broadcast that. Or to stand in the way of the railroad. In fact, I'd like to agree a right of way from the range to the Gauntsville valley.'

'Without which everything else is meaningless,' Smith said drily. 'How much?'

'Twenty-five thousand dollars.'

Reese almost exploded. Smith only put a finger to his pursed lips. Then:

'Ten thousand in cash, the rest in stock.'

'Half in cash, the rest in debentures,' Rhodes said.

'Agreed,' Smith said. 'But we'd like you to leave the valley. Less talk that way.'

Rhodes nodded. 'One more thing. You might like to see this.' He reached into his pocket and pulled out a paper which he handed to Smith. 'It's my last will and testament, a notarized copy of which has been sent to The Northern Wilderness Railroad Company.'

'Why?' Reese asked.

'Because he leaves everything to it,' Smith said. 'Our chief competitors. If anything were to happen to Mr Rhodes, they'd own the right of way. They could stop us dead, leave us holding the vast tracts of unsaleable land. And it would cost them nothing to do it.'

'Our stock would sink to zero!' Reese said, horrified.

'Precisely,' Smith said.

'It's fortunate for you I'm hale and hearty,' Rhodes said. 'When I get my money I intend to get married and take my bride to San Francisco. The valley has bad memories for both of us.'

'What's that to us?' Reese asked.

Smith frowned at his legal ignorance. 'A marriage makes all previous wills void,' he told him shortly. 'And the ranch?'

'I'm going to give it to a . . . cousin of mine, Jake Miles. He'll give you no problems. Even sell you horses, good ones.'

'We'll meet in the bank in an hour,' Smith said decisively, standing up. 'I'm tempted to offer you a job, Mr Rhodes. Even a seat on the board.'

Rhodes rose too. 'I think not, Mr Smith. You play too rough for me.'

We do hope that you have enjoyed reading this large print book.

Did you know that all of our titles are available for purchase?

We publish a wide range of high quality large print books including:
Romances, Mysteries, Classics
General Fiction
Non Fiction and Westerns

Special interest titles available in large print are:
The Little Oxford Dictionary
Music Book, Song Book
Hymn Book, Service Book

Also available from us courtesy of Oxford University Press:
Young Readers' Dictionary
(large print edition)
Young Readers' Thesaurus
(large print edition)

For further information or a free brochure, please contact us at:
Ulverscroft Large Print Books Ltd.,
The Green, Bradgate Road, Anstey,
Leicester, LE7 7FU, England.
Tel: (00 44) **0116 236 4325**
Fax: (00 44) **0116 234 0205**

Other titles in the
Linford Western Library:

A TOWN CALLED TROUBLESOME

John Dyson

Matt Matthews had carved his ranch out of the wild Wyoming frontier. But he had his troubles. The big blow of '86 was catastrophic, with dead beeves littering the plains, and the oncoming winter presaged worse. On top of this, a gang of desperadoes had moved into the Snake River valley, killing, raping and rustling. All Matt can do is to take on the killers single-handed. But will he escape the hail of lead?

GAMBLER'S BULLETS

Robert Lane

The conquering of the American west threw up men with all the virtues and vices. The men of vision, ready to work hard to build a better life, were in the majority. But there were also work-shy gamblers, robbers and killers. Amongst these ne'er-do-wells were Melvyn Revett, Trevor Younis and Wilf Murray. But two determined men — Curtis Tyson and Neville Gough — took to the trail, and not until their last bullets were spent would they give up the fight against the lawless trio.

MIDNIGHT LYNCHING

Terry Murphy

When Ruby Malone's husband is lynched by a sheriff's posse, Wells Fargo investigator Asa Harker goes after the beautiful widow expecting her to lead him to the vast sum of money stolen from his company. But Ruby has gone on the outlaw trail with the handsome, young Ben Whitman. Worse still, Harker finds he must deal with a crooked sheriff. Without help, it looks as if he will not only fail to recover the stolen money but also lose his life into the bargain.

THE WIND WAGON

Troy Howard

Sheriff Al Corning was as tough as they came and with his four seasoned deputies he kept the peace in Laramie — at least until the squatters came. To fend off starvation, the settlers took some cattle off the cowmen, including Jonas Lefler. A hard, unforgiving man, Lefler retaliated with lynchings. Things got worse when one of the squatters revealed he was a former Texas lawman — and no mean shooter. Could Sheriff Corning prevent further bloodshed?